SOLVING PECULIAR CRIMES

Radine Trees Nehring

ST KITTS PRESS • WICHITA, KS

PUBLISHED BY ST KITTS PRESS
PO Box 8173   Wichita, KS 67208
316-641-0506   diana@skpub.com

Edited by Diana Tillison
Cover illustration by Ron Muhlenbruch

First Edition 2020

Library of Congress Cataloging-in-Publication Data

Names: Nehring, Radine Trees, [date]- author. | Mystery fiction. gsafd
Title: Solving peculiar crimes / Radine Trees Nehring.
Description: First edition. | Wichita, KS : St Kitts Press, 2020. |
  Summary: "Carrie and Henry encounter peculiar crimes in these stories
  featuring right, wrong, and redemption. Carrie's urge to help people who
  are in trouble often draws her into puzzling and sometimes dangerous
  human events. Henry provides support and back-up when her curiosity and
  helpful nature expose both of them to trouble and danger. Carrie McCrite
  and Henry King are the protagonists in Nehring's popular "To Die For"
  Mystery Series"-- Provided by publisher.
Identifiers: LCCN 2020044689 (print) | LCCN 2020044690 (ebook) | ISBN
  9781931206075 (trade paperback) | ISBN 9781931206082 (epub)
Subjects: LCGFT: Short stories.
Classification: LCC PS3614.E44 S58 2020 (print) | LCC PS3614.E44 (ebook)
  | DDC 813/.6--dc23
LC record available at https://lccn.loc.gov/2020044689
LC ebook record available at https://lccn.loc.gov/2020044690

A THANK YOU NOTE

Arkansas, "The Natural State," is full of locations that almost demand to be shared with the world. Each location that has become a springboard for one of my mystery stories has a lot of fans who, like me, are eager for everyone to know just why their special place is, well, special! The kindness and enthusiasm of these fans—my wonderful research assistants— feeds into the writing I share with you in my novels and short stories. More than one of them has become so involved in my research that he or she has said some version of, "Oh, Radine, look up there. Couldn't we use that as a...?" Others have startled (and pleased) me by publicly showcasing a novel featuring their place.

But however much my books are devoted to the Arkansas landscape, they are still mainly mystery puzzles about crime solving that often lead to redemption of one or more characters featured in each story. For me, that's one of the best features in any author's traditional mystery writing.

Dedicated to John A. Nehring,
my long-time life companion and best friend
(1933-2019)

CHAPTERS

THE HANGING

"...you will hang by the neck until dead; and may God have mercy on your soul."

The records showed seventy-nine men died here after hearing those words in Judge Parker's courtroom.

Carrie McCrite blinked as the early morning sun glared off the freshly painted board fence surrounding the gallows. Why did that fence have to be so pure looking, so clean and white? It seemed fake, like a stage set.

Next to her, in the aisle seat, Beth swung into part two of her story, *Granddaughter Megan's visit to the Tulsa Zoo*. Carrie knew the words by heart since this was the third—no, fourth—retelling and, staring out the trolley window, she mouthed the final lines as Beth spoke them, "and my clever granddaughter said 'Mama, the baby lion just pooped. Why doesn't he have diapers on?'"

Beth took a deep breath and, before she could

begin the story of Megan's first day at kindergarten—
third re-telling—Carrie tapped a finger on the
window and said, "Oh, look over there, Beth. What
is that?"

"Huh?"

Carrie pointed at the high board fence, which,
now that she thought about it, looked like a
mammoth enclosure for trash containers.

The tourist trolley turned toward a parking space
as Carrie said, "See there? Looks like the trash
containment fence at McDonald's, but worlds bigger."

"Gallows," said Beth, not missing a beat as she
switched topics. "We have flyers about it at our
information center. Don't you have them at yours?
Hung almost a hundred men in there, murders and
rapiers and..."

Carrie said, "Rapists," without thinking.

"Well, rapists, rapiers, whatever. Anyway, you
know what they did. Raping and killing were crimes
you got hung for here and, by golly, Judge Isaac
Parker, who's still called 'The Hanging Judge' today,
saw to it that you were hung."

"Hanged," said Carrie. "Weren't there juries who
made the decision of guilt or innocence? Judge
Parker merely applied punishment as the law pre-

scribed. He didn't make the laws."

"Well, hanged then, and hang it, Carrie, if you know so much, why ask me? If you don't know, well, quit interrupting and pay attention to what I'm saying so you might learn something."

Beth made a huffing sound before she went on. "Yes, of course they had juries and a really, really terrible jail. 'Hell on the Border' it was called. It's in those buildings over there; you'll see it all in a few minutes. My goodness, I'd have thought you paid more attention to the information they gave us about this trip, not to mention read the tourist flyers from the racks in your center. Judge Parker was the dispenser of law over all those outlaws that hid out in Indian Territory. Across the river is where they escaped in those days, and I tell you that was an awful thing for those poor Indians. See there," she pointed past Carrie's shoulder, "over the Arkansas River. Parker sent U. S. Marshalls to capture the meanest, terribilist outlaws at risk of life and limb."

Carrie, still looking out the window, smiled to herself. She knew the history quite well, but at least Beth had stopped her Megan stories.

Another breathy huff before Beth said, "Did I tell you about Megan's first day in kindergarten? It is such a cute story. You'll love it. My daughter dressed her in a new pink—oh, oh, I guess we're getting out now. I have photos to show you later."

The trolley had come to a full stop in front of the Ft. Smith National Historic Site, and seventeen Arkansas Tourist Information Center employees rose as one, eager to be out in the glorious September day. They'd boarded the tourist trolley at dawn, when most of them were barely awake. Now the early sunshine beckoned to everyone taking part in what Carrie considered the most ponderously named event in all of Arkansas, "The Arkansas Department of Parks and Tourism's Fall Tourist Information Center Familiarization Tour." No wonder it had been dubbed "Fam Tour" long before Carrie went to work for the department.

Wonderful idea, though, since travel hosts who went on the tours could speak with experience when they told people traveling in Arkansas about the many things to enjoy.

As she moved down the trolley aisle, Carrie yawned. Their visit to the National Historic Site did begin early, but this was usual for the tours. The real problem was that Beth's chatter not only went on all day, it extended far into the night. Since each of them managed a center on an entrance highway in Benton County, Tour Director Adam Yost's understandable decision had been to pair them as roommates.

Next time Adam can room with her, Carrie thought, grinning as she pictured it.

She was in front of Beth who, still gabbing about Megan's school clothes, came down the steps too quickly. She tripped and fell against Carrie, knocking her to the ground and smashing down on top of her.

"OOOOF. Well, sorry, but you should have moved out of the way faster." The shrill voice rang painfully in Carrie's ears as she tried to catch her breath and straighten her twisted leg.

Beth, whose fall had been broken by Carrie's body, was quickly lifted and pulled away. Then several women bent over Carrie, their voices clanging in her ears. "Are you hurt?" "Shouldn't we call 911?" "Oh, look at your poor jacket." "Here's her shoe, under the trolley." "Should somebody call an ambulance?"

Carrie struggled to fill her empty lungs with air and gather her wits. Finally, blessed relief, the clanging stopped, and Adam Yost knelt beside her, his deep tones a welcome contrast to the shrill female voices. As she pushed herself off the ground, Adam took one of her hands in his and put an arm around her shoulders to help her lift into a sitting position.

Carrie would have laughed had she been able to

manage it. If her seat companion was seeing this, she'd be wild with jealousy. After five years as a widow, Carrie was content alone, but Beth, divorced for three years, made it clear to all she was shopping for her next husband. The current target? Their handsome tour director.

Sensibility began to return quickly after Carrie sat up, but she realized her ankle was currently in no mood to support her. There was some compensation, however, for she couldn't hear Beth's voice any more. Maybe they'd leave her in the trolley to recover—after Adam quit poking about all over her body, that is.

"Ooooo, ahhh, haha. Sorry, Adam. I'm ticklish there."

Yes, if Beth was anywhere near, she'd be livid.

"Um, just wanted to be sure that, um, nothing was broken. I do have EMT training and—oh, excuse me, Carrie, just checking for damage there." He sat back, removing his hands from her body. "I don't feel anything out of place. Some swelling in that ankle, though. We should get an x-ray."

"If you don't mind, I'd like to just get back in the trolley and rest. You go on with the group. I've visited this site quite recently anyway."

"Well, should I ask Beth to stay with..."

"No! That is, no, thanks. I'll be fine alone."

Was that a wink?

He said, "Are you sure? Do your ribs feel okay? Any trouble breathing? Any pain? Beth is quite a bit heavier and, oh, I mean, Beth did come down on you rather heavily."

She managed a smile and shook her head. "Beth just knocked the breath out of me, that's all."

Finally, undoubtedly remembering the tight schedule they were committed to, Adam helped her to her seat in the trolley and, after promising x-rays would be available when they reached the Fayetteville stop, he hurried off to join his charges.

Carrie, with her feet propped on the reversed seat in front of her, shut her eyes to enjoy the silence and whisper a prayer.

Eventually she opened her eyes and looked at her watch. *Oh, goodness, I must have dozed off.*

She glanced out the window to see if her group was anywhere around. There was no one in sight. They had probably gone inside the building that served initially as an army barracks and then, from 1875 until 1896, to house Judge Isaac Parker's Federal Court for the Western District of Arkansas. Carrie hadn't mentioned it to anyone except Adam, but she really had been here recently, only four months ago, in fact. She, her friend Henry King, and neighbors Eleanor and Jason Stack came down Highway 49 one Saturday to go antiquing in nearby Van Buren and tour this historic site. It was, after all, only a little more than an hour's drive from home.

The gallows fence caught her attention again. Who could miss it with all that white paint? Sort of socked you in the face. Spooky place, but effective as a dramatic display. Kids would probably love it. Well, it was one way to teach history, and the more noticeable the better for the purpose, she supposed.

She daydreamed then, picturing the inside of the courtroom building and jails as she had seen them last spring. In her mind she was walking there again, trying to understand what it had been like all those years ago. She'd even thought about lying down on one of the pallets in the original stone dungeon. She shut her eyes again, imagining the sandpaper roughness of the wool blanket, reconstructing sounds and smells as they must have been when the place was full of unwashed men, not to mention the open buckets that served as toilets. Talk about re-enacting history. She could smell it.

Huh? What was that? Movement up on the gallows brought her back to the present. Oh, ugh, how awful. For some stupid reason, they'd displayed a dummy as if it were being hanged. Maybe that was in honor of their tour. She looked away. That was too much realism as far as she was concerned. Ghoulish. A terrible way to die, but then great agony had been inflicted on others by the hundred and sixty men who'd been sentenced to hang here. Of those, only seventy-nine were actually brought to the rope, each one duly convicted of rape or murder. Surely they didn't deserve her sympathy.

Had any innocent men been hanged? Probably. It did happen, though maybe it had been less likely in Judge Parker's court.

She turned back toward the gallows and, as she did, the dummy swung slightly. It was hanging free, so the trap door had been sprung.

As she watched, hypnotized by the slow oscillation of the body, something moved near the wall behind the gallows. The movement turned into a man dressed entirely in white.

The trolley was parked parallel to one side of the board enclosure so she could see the slope of the half-roof over the gallows, the gallows framework, the knotted rope, and the white hair on the head of the dummy. She remembered that there was a small door in the stone wall behind the gallows platform; she'd noticed it when she was here last June. It was opposite the wide spectators' opening at the front that tourists used today and was, therefore, hidden from the main buildings. That had probably been where prisoners were brought in before each hanging and where their bodies were taken out after. She'd assumed the smaller door was locked these days, but evidently not. The man dressed in white had used it.

Her eyes lifted to the rope again, and a chill spiked down her backbone. Awful. Why would they...what poor taste...terrible image, even for their adult tour group. And why an old man with white hair and a beard? If the face weren't so long and thin it would look like they'd hanged Santa Claus.

She was going to have to speak to someone about this.

Carrie kept her eyes on the man now standing behind the gallows enclosure. Maybe he was lighting a cigarette. Was he hiding behind the wall so he could smoke? As she watched, the man in white started walking toward the parking lot. He paused a moment to look around, then began to run. Good thing the trolley windows were tinted. He couldn't see her watching.

This was so peculiar, like a stage play with only two characters—a swinging dummy and the man in a white jacket, white pants, white sneakers, white ball cap, white gloves.

Oh. Maybe he worked in food service somewhere.

Then Carrie realized that, even if this man had been up on the gallows platform while she was watching, she probably wouldn't have seen him against the white walls.

He stopped running and turned to look back at the gallows. For a moment he appeared frozen, but whirled toward the parking lot as a carload of tourists pulled in. He began running again, changing direction to avoid the tourists, heading straight toward the trolley.

Carrie struggled to get her feet under her and walk. How did you close the doors? She had seen the driver operate a lever. Only four or five hobbles and she could reach it.

Too late. She sank down as far as she could in her seat as the man jumped through the rear door, breathing heavily. Unless he came toward the front he might not see her.

Silence. What was he *doing?*

She heard the voices of the people from the car fading away as they headed toward the welcome center. There was a soft shuffling of the man's feet and she tensed, wondering if she should bolt out the front door in spite of the problem ankle.

His breathing sounded uneven, but it was slowing. He felt so close, as if he were right next to her. Was he moving forward?

Then there was a new sound. She strained to identify it. Sniffing and a throaty whine. The man was crying!

She had to look and risked turning her head for a peek between the seats. He was standing by the back door, and she could see the side of his face clearly, an old face, showing, she thought, great sorrow, not evil.

The sobbing stopped; there was a sniff and blow, then silence returned. Carrie was sure now that he hadn't seen her. There had been no action to indicate he knew any living person was nearby.

He was statue quiet, his head bowed. After a couple of moments she heard him speak what sounded like a name, "Alison."

Then, in an instant, it was over. A quick thunk of rubber sole on the step and he was running down the street toward a large black van facing away from the parking lot.

Carrie stood and, holding onto seat backs, walked to the rear door so she could read the van's license plate. The letters and numbers were from Arkansas. The man in white got in the passenger side of the van. It started, raced around the corner, and was gone. So there had been a driver, waiting.

Carrie limped back up the aisle, took the note pad out of her tote, and wrote down the letters and numbers she had seen on the license. Now what? Go find someone?

If only she had a cane.

Then she remembered her phone and looked in the stack of flyers to find the number of the park office. Bingo!

That was when the real action started, a stage play seen from Carrie's front row seat. Before long two uniformed park rangers hurried out of the main building, ran down the sidewalk and into the gallows enclosure. In a moment Carrie could see their heads and shoulders on the gallows platform. Agitation. Action. The dummy began dropping. They were handling it as gently as if it had been...had been...

Oh, dear God! Surely it wasn't real.

In the blink of an eye the police came, no sirens. Then a plain black car slid into the space next to the trolley. A man in a dark suit got out and headed down the walkway toward the office. Probably the FBI since they were in a National Park.

No sign of her tour group yet, but plenty going on out here for her to watch.

She sat alone for only another moment. Two police officers, a man and a woman, entered the trolley and perched on seats across from her. They introduced themselves, then asked what she had seen. She told them everything. Almost. She said nothing about a license number or the name Alison. After all, how could she know that the sad man had done something wrong?

After she had finished her story, there was silence. They weren't offering to tell her anything, so she asked, "Was it...was it a real person?"

More silence, then, "Yes."

"Who? Do you know?"

They glanced at each other before the man said, "Judge Benjamin Carriden. He'd been retired for more than twenty years. He was very old."

"Oh, no, no. Then I saw a real hanging."

They looked at each other again, at their feet, back at her. The woman said, "Well, not exactly. The Judge's funeral is scheduled for later today. He died Thursday. The funeral home says the Judge had requested a closed coffin and everything was ready, so they didn't know the coffin was empty."

All three of them turned as if their heads were pulled on invisible strings. They stared at the gallows, more difficult to look at now because the white boards glared furiously in the mid-morning sun.

Finally Carrie said, "But how did someone get him up there?"

"There was a wheelchair left beside the gallows steps. He had been very frail. Didn't weigh much."

"Why, why would anyone do this?"

The woman answered quickly, as if she'd already been thinking about it. "A guess? More than one of the Judge's cases was controversial. He was a stickler for proper collection and preservation of evidence. Sometimes defendants were set free, no matter how certain their guilt had seemed. Evidence thrown out. He went strictly by the book. Didn't set well with some folks."

"Those controversial cases, do you know anything about them?"

"I know some," the woman said. "They all happened before my time, but we studied them at the academy as examples of how not to collect and safeguard evidence. Bad examples, so to speak. Learn from your mistakes. That sort of thing."

She hesitated, staring out of the trolley's front window, then spoke as if she had memorized the words. "There was the murder of John Akin—alleged murder, of course. Then the murder of Lily Will-banks, the rape and murder of Mary Anna Macon, and the murder of Harrison McDougal. Those were the four main cases we studied, the worst examples, where guilt of the defendants seemed definite. Ever heard of any of them?"

"I'm not from around here," Carrie said. Then, after a pause, she asked, "What about the accused people, the possibly guilty ones who went free as a result of Judge Carriden's rulings?"

"Well, in the Akin case, the defendant just disappeared. It was thought he left the country. Willbanks's murderer killed again, and everyone worked very hard to make sure that case was airtight. He went to prison.

"About ten years ago Mary Anna Macon's killer raped and strangled a young woman named Alison Bailey. He's sitting in a cell on death row. As for the man alleged to have killed Harrison Johns, he's been a model citizen ever since. He's about 70 now and, so far as I know, is enjoying his children and grand-children."

"I see." And she did see.

After asking a few more questions, they left her alone. Carrie watched the activity outside for several more minutes until, at last, a hearse came, and the body of Judge Benjamin Carriden went off to its final resting place.

Carrie opened her Bible and sat reading it for what seemed like a long, peaceful time before the tour group returned.

Beth bounced in, and it was obvious neither she nor anyone else in the group knew of the drama that had unfolded on the gallows while they toured a legendary jail and courtroom. They had also heard the life story of Judge Isaac Parker, who once said he didn't make the laws, only enforced them and, by some reports, also said he didn't believe in capital punishment.

The trolley started moving while Beth began droning an account of their tour, and Carrie stared down at the license plate number on her note pad. Then she turned the pad over and stuck it in her tote bag.

She shut her eyes, thinking about the man who had cried for Alison Bailey. Her father? Whoever he was, she hoped he had found peace.

CRIME GOES ON A HONEYMOON

Carrie had always awakened quickly, whether it was to teen thoughts about a school day, concerns about problem-solving for her job, or to baby Rob howling that he was hungry. Through all her years until now, whether in dark or at dawn, she had come awake, eyes opening wide, to anticipate whatever the day would unfold for her.

This morning was very different. Afraid to open her eyes, afraid she was dreaming, she thought her way along her body, checking. Ummm, no, last night was no dream.

The ivory satin dress Shirley had made for her. A wedding ceremony. Rob giving her away to Henry. Cake and a buffet. Laughter with family and good friends, and finally coming to this room in The Crescent Hotel with Henry, her new husband.

Honeymoon Suite. Ummm.

She clamped her teeth together to stop a giggle. Sex with Amos, her first husband, had been business-like, if that term could possibly fit such activity, and had stopped altogether once Rob was conceived. With Henry, her new husband, she finally understood what she supposed many couples of any age beyond puberty already knew quite well.

Carrie rolled over slowly to face the man in bed next to her. Henry was on his side, turned away from her, his bare back mostly out of the covers. The identifying scar was there, next to his shoulder, the result of a gun in the hands of a teenage killer he was preparing to arrest. The bullet's entry scar, high on Henry's chest, had missed everything they called vital.

Henry's gun had not missed, and the mental scar of killing a boy, even though that boy had just killed a convenience store clerk and turned his gun on Henry, was much worse than the marks she had touched so gently last night.

That trauma had led to his retirement from police work as soon as he was eligible and to his eventual divorce and move to Arkansas. Good triumphing over evil? Carrie hoped he saw it that way.

She resisted a temptation to bounce and wondered if Henry would awaken at any movement from her. She could go shower and return to bed. Then, maybe...

He stirred and rolled to face her.

"Morning," she said.

"Yep, and our first day as an old married couple."

"Who you callin' old?" She slid toward her husband, pushing her body to touch his – all the way down.

The heat of newly discovered sexual pleasure was surprising and wonderful, but eventually hunger spoke loudly too and, showered and dressed, Henry and Carrie walked sedately into the Crescent Dining Room for a late breakfast.

After they'd eaten, the server cleared the table and put plates holding small heart-shaped cakes with red icing in front of each of them.

"A gift for newlyweds from the hotel," their server said, smiling. "Whatever your age, you qualify."

Ignoring what she considered the server's unnecessary concession that newlyweds could be their age, Carrie said, "Oh, they look delicious," and took a bite out of her cake.

In a moment she opened her mouth and spit the cake bite into her empty coffee cup, spit again, looked at the two men staring at her, and said, "Wha? OOo." She stuck out her tongue and leaned toward her husband. "Hin-ee, p-oh-ow-u."

He looked closely at her tongue, then said, "Cara, don't swallow. Keep your mouth open and your tongue out.

"Quick," he said to the server without looking away from Carrie's mouth, "bring me tweezers if you have them or pointed blade pliers. If you can't find those, maybe an ice pick or something with a flat, narrow blade. Tweezers best. Looks like there was an open staple in the cake. It's stuck in her tongue."

The server stood, staring at him. Henry said, much more sharply, "Go find those tweezers," before the man finally hurried away.

He touched Carrie's hand. "Sit still, Little Love, we'll have it out in a minute."

It took several minutes, but eventually their server returned and handed tweezers to Henry. "One of the servers had these in her purse. I sterilized them in our kitchen. Should I call the manager?"

Henry took the tweezers, reached in Carrie's open mouth, pulled a staple out of her tongue. "Of all the...Cara, go wash your mouth out now. A powerful mouthwash. If you need, use mine. Are you otherwise okay? No more staples?"

"I'm fine, except for a pricked tongue. Thank goodness I didn't swallow."

He stood when she did, then turned away quickly and grabbed the arm of the server, who was starting to remove Carrie's coffee cup and the cakes from the table. "No, leave all that here for me to look through."

He sat, broke his cake apart, poked at it, and pulled out three open staples. He then took a spoon, looked through Carrie's coffee cup and, with an oath, picked out two staples. Mashing both cakes exposed more staples.

"I think you had better call the manager. Were these cakes baked in your kitchen?"

"N-nu-no, a local bakery brings them in. We order them for all our honeymoon couples. I'll, uh, get the manager."

Carrie had returned by the time the manager came, and they both stared at the staples Henry had laid out on a napkin.

"I have no idea how this happened, Mr. Russell, and I..."

Henry interrupted him. "Russell? Were these cakes made for a couple named Russell? We are not that couple. Do you mark the cakes for specific couples?"

The man wobbled, fell into the chair across from Henry, and put his head in his hands for a few moments before he looked up. "No, not normally. We often have honeymoon couples staying here so we keep a stock of cakes, all alike, to give out. But the bakery delivery man said last night these cakes were made especially for the Russells. I supposed they were sugar-free, gluten-free, or some such, and I put them in a box with a label for the Russells on top. I don't usually get involved in serving our diners." He glared at the server. "Our staff usually handles that very well."

"This was the only set of cakes left in the kitchen," the server said. "I assumed, therefore, that this was the Russell couple. Maybe the Russells were here earlier and had left before I came on duty. I suppose their server didn't see your label."

"Okay, but right now go to the front desk and find out if there's a couple named Russell staying here. And, sir, madam, I apologize deeply. We will be glad to comp all your meals as long as you stay with us."

"We will allow you to pay for this breakfast," Henry said. "And I suggest you now call the police."

* * *

"*Staples?*" Detective Gloria Wolverton stared at the spread of u-shaped metal loops on the napkin. "Bizarre, but of course they could be damaging, especially if swallowed. Might need to be surgically removed."

"But not life-threatening for the most part," said Henry, "though, as my wife can tell you, painful and potentially dangerous all the same."

"Meant for some newlywed couple named Russell?"

"Yes," said the manager. "They stayed with us last night but checked out right after eating an early breakfast this morning. These cakes were labeled for them but, due to a mistake by the server, they got the wrong ones."

"Do you know where the Russells were headed?"

A young woman stepped out of the group now standing just beyond the table. "I checked them out. The man said they needed to get to the Northwest Arkansas airport in time for a flight." She hesitated, then added, "Maybe I kind of imagined it but I thought he seemed pretty short-tempered. In fact, I remember thinking I was glad I wasn't married to him. His wife was, well, kind of plain. Plain dress. Very quiet. She stood behind him looking at the floor and said nothing."

"He didn't mention a specific flight?"

"No."

"Okay. What's your name?"

"Robyn Talbott."

"Thanks, Ms. Talbott. Please go to the table by the window. Officer Diaz will give you a pen and paper. Write down all you can remember about how the Russells looked and acted. Their ages, hair color, what they were wearing, anything like that. Do it as quickly as you can. I'd like to catch up with them before they get on a plane and, with your help, we can give the airport staff their descriptions and, perhaps, have them detained. Will their home address and other information be at the front desk?"

"Yes, Ms., uh, detective."

"Good. Please put your contact information on the paper when you're finished. We may need to ask you more questions later."

A woman wearing a hotel housekeeper's uniform moved from the back of the group. "I maybe can help. I am Isobelle, housekeeping. I saw them when they were here. I saw their clothing when they left."

"That will help. Thank you, Isobelle. The officer will give you something to write on as well. Sit at another table and don't compare notes with Robyn. Put your name and contact information on your paper, please.

"Anyone else here remember seeing either of the Russells other than their server here in the dining room?"

"Who's on the front desk now?" the manager asked.

Robyn stopped writing. "Derek."

"Did he see the Russells?"

"No, but I told him what was happening after the detective said I was needed in here, and I called him to take over for me."

Detective Wolverton nodded an affirmation and asked the manager the name, phone number, and address of the supplier of the cakes. She wrote the information down, pulled out her phone, and left the room.

Henry leaned close to Carrie and said, "Hope she's gone to ask someone at the station to get over to the bakery before the person there who's responsible for the Russells' cakes finds out that the staples missed their target."

Carrie smiled. "I'd love to be a fly on the bakery wall when the police arrive there." She pointed to a quiet area at the back of the dining room. "Let's move over there so we can talk."

After a few minutes of silence while the two hotel employees thought and wrote, and Carrie and Henry moved away from their breakfast table, a man pushed through the closed dining room doors, looked around, then said to Officer Diaz, "You're interested in people named Russell?"

"Yes. Do you have information about them?"

"You bet. Mr. Russell is at the front desk, and he's mighty angry. Says he came back to get two little cakes he was supposed to be given this morning. Says he got the wrong ones. I said I'd get his cakes. So, what should I do?"

Officer Diaz said, "Russell's come back? That's peculiar. He sure wants those cakes. Okay, I'll get the detective. For now, you stay here. The detective and I will talk with him."

Carrie looked at Henry and spoke quietly. "Do you suppose Russell knows about the staples and wants to avoid an uproar?"

"No, but I bet something else was supposed to be inside those cakes. What do you think about something small – like maybe diamonds?" He grinned and shook his head. "What a surprise. This is becoming quite interesting. The fact Russell came back is highly suspicious. I am sorry you got spiked, but that opened up the mystery. Since you're okay, it's become entertaining and, for once, we're only observers. I wonder what they'll find at that bakery. Someone there had to be part of whatever the plot is."

"Um hm, certainly. And I'd say rubies. The red cakes, you know."

Just then Detective Wolverton came back into the room, bringing a fuming man with her. "What is this? All I want are the two red cakes I know were intended for me."

The detective led him to the table where Carrie and Henry had been eating. "You needed some staples?"

The man stared at the mess on the table. "Staples? What is this?"

"Another couple got your cakes by mistake. They were filled with staples. Very dangerous."

Russell jerked away from her, swearing, and rushed toward the dining room doors. Henry stood and hurried after him, but Officer Diaz quickly reached out to grab the man, and Detective Wolverton clipped handcuffs on his wrists as she said, "You were, perhaps, expecting something a little more valuable than staples?" She turned to Derek. "Where's his wife?"

Russell blew out a string of swear words. "That b...is not my wife, just some woman hired for the weekend. I left her in the car park and have no intention of going back to pick her up."

The detective took out her phone again.

Henry whispered, "Guess she's calling for help. Hope someone got to the bakery in time to stop the person who made the cakes."

Carrie, who usually had an amateur detective's interest in any crime, said, "We can find out what happened later. For now, let's go back to our room. We have time for, well, for time alone."

Henry laughed. "This is certainly a new you. What is it? You don't have any person here who's been wronged or is in danger to get involved with?"

She said, "Nope. I have a husband to get involved with." They both stood, Carrie spoke briefly with the detective, got a nod, and the newlyweds walked out of the room.

* * *

Postscript: Carrie was right. The cakes were supposed to conceal stolen rubies.

SOMETHING EXTRA FOR CHRISTMAS

The door of the house closed behind them. *Ka-chunk.*

Henry let go of his suitcase handle, glanced at Carrie, and said, "Well," as he thought, *This is going to take some getting used to.*

Carrie was stuck in an embarrassing and uncharacteristic silence since she didn't want to say what was bouncing inside her head. *Everything is going to be okay. I am happy to have this man in my home. I had room for Henry's clothes in my extra closet. There are tools, fishing rods, boots, plus goodness knows what else in mysterious boxes on shelves in the garage. What was mine or his is now ours.*

Fishing rods? A laugh burst out before she could control it.

Since laughter can be infectious, Henry laughed with her and they came together for a hug.

Henry's question, "What now?" spoken above her head, ended the laughter as well as the hug. *Good, he's not going to ask what's funny.*

"Now? Christmas! Golly, Henry, our wedding and honeymoon put me way behind on Christmas, but since you're here to help, we can make it. Please take our bags to the bedroom while I check mail, then let's change to clothes more comfortable for work in the basement.

"Oh, wait! Sorry, I didn't think. Do you have any Christmas decorations in those boxes in the garage?"

He shook his head. "Irena hired out seasonal decorating, and this humble cop wasn't invited to participate. But, of course, the money was hers, so she had the say about most everything, including Christmas. What I brought here is mostly what I took with me when we divorced. Personal stuff."

Carrie's eyes suddenly felt wet behind her glasses, and she turned away for a moment before she said, "I understand, and never mind. I have plenty of Christmas decorations to share with you. That means sharing half the chores, too. First, let's bring up our Christmas tree and decorate it. Then there are angels and a crèche to go on the mantel and the wreath for the door and, well, I'm sure glad you're here. Later this week we begin our Christmas shopping but, for now, off to the basement, husband dear."

* * *

The mall parking lot was almost full even though

it was early on a Tuesday morning, but crowds didn't bother Carrie so, with Henry following, she pushed her way into stores as they checked off gift items on their hastily made list. After selecting a sweater and a book for her son Rob, and a necklace for Henry's daughter that she liked well enough to covet, she said, "That's everyone on our list. Oh, look, an empty bench across the hall. Let's head for it and hope no one else decides to sit there first."

Holding her purse and a gift box in front of her like a shield, she squeezed between a woman carrying two large shopping bags and a boy whose ragged jeans would surely fall off at any moment. *Kids!*

Henry – almost a foot taller than either the encumbered woman or the boy – followed along easily while people glanced at him and hurried out of his way. He sat next to Carrie and put their shopping bags on the floor at his feet while Santa ho-ho'd from his throne across the mall concourse and *Deck the Halls* changed to *Jingle Bells.* The boy in drooping pants stopped walking and leaned against a wall, staring at Santa, who was now putting a "Gone to Lunch" sign on his easel.

Henry said, "That kid sure looks sad. Kids these days can sometimes look glum but, especially at Christmas, it seems peculiar. How old do you think he is, maybe twelve or thirteen?"

"Yes, I'd guess that. I'd like to give him a hug. I bet he's wishing he was young enough to tell Santa what he wants for Christmas."

They sat in silence, letting voices and Christmas carols fill the air space. Finally, Henry asked, "Should I take this load to the car before we continue, or are we ready to leave?"

Carrie came back from private prayers and looked away from the boy with the sad face. "I think we're done. We can do gift certificates for the mail carrier and the woman who delivers our newspaper."

"What about us?"

"Oh, yes." She smiled up at him. "But we'll need to shop alone, won't we? We can do that later."

"Why not now? We drove twenty-five miles to get to this mall. How about you pick a store where you want me to shop and I'll pick one for you? Then we'll split up."

"That's a brilliant idea. We can begin a McCrite and King Christmas tradition right now. Picking stores."

"Okay. But how about I take this load of stuff to the car before I shop? I'll pick that store across the mall for me. The Outdoor Store. Now, you tell me where to shop."

"I pick Jewelry Boutique."

"What? Not Kitchen Specialties?"

She glared at him and saw his grin.

"Okay, my dear, no electric noodle maker for you. Meet you back here in, what? Thirty minutes?"

"I may need a little longer—how about up to forty-five minutes? The one who has to wait will have fun watching Santa and the children. If someone has taken our bench we can always lean against the wall."

"Good. See you in forty-five minutes. Outdoor Store, remember." Henry hoisted packages and disappeared in the crowd. Carrie headed for the Outdoor Store.

She was at the store's entrance when a loud bang sounded behind her. Then, before she could process what she'd heard, there was a second explosive BANG followed by shouts and screams.

NO! Those were gunshots!

She started to duck into the store, but then the cry of one female voice grew louder than every other noise. "Tommyeee. My baby. Tommyeee."

Hearing that, Carrie no longer considered ducking or hiding. She turned and saw people running in every direction or crouching and crawling. Every one of them seemed to be shrieking for help or the police or for some person. A teenage girl was yelling for her mother.

But, above it all, Carrie still heard the cries of the woman who was on her knees in front of Santa's throne.

On the throne—his slender form outlined against a painted snow scene—sat the glum boy. His left arm circled a toddler with blood on his cheek. The teen boy's right hand was shaking, which made the gun it held wobble wildly.

Oh, merciful God, oh, Prince of Peace...a child...two children, really. Dear God. A mere baby.

She imagined Henry's voice inside her head: *Stay away. Extreme danger. Erratic shooter. You could end up dead at any second. Danger, danger, danger. Let the law handle this.*

But he was only a toddler. Probably not even two yet. He hadn't a clue to what was happening or why Mommy wasn't holding him.

People continued scattering, crawling, shouting into their phones. Feeling like an automaton, Carrie walked toward the tableau – a mother, a boy, and a baby.

"Stay away," the boy shouted. "If anyone comes close, I can shoot this kid."

Only a baby. His little blue overalls have dark spots on the front. Blood?

"Hello," Carrie said to the boy with the gun.

The Lord is my light and my help. Whom shall I fear. Whom shall I fear?

"He's just a baby," she said to the boy. "If you give him to his mother, I will come and sit with you. You don't need a little kid." She thought of Henry's grandson Johnny, about the same age as this baby with the smear of blood on his cheek. He wasn't making a sound, but he was certainly conscious. His eyes were wide open. Why wasn't he crying? Could babies go into shock?

"NO, stay away."

"I'd like to talk with you, hear what you have to say."

"Heard enough talk."

"I want you to tell me your story. Tell me why you're sitting in Santa's chair holding a baby."

"Because...because then they can't make me."

"No, they can't," she said. *Oh God, give me the right things to say. Tell me what is behind this tragedy.*

The toddler's mother was now lying on the floor, sobbing.

"I will listen to you," Carrie said. "I need to understand why people want to make you do something you don't like."

"LIKE? I hate it. I hate him."

"Him?"

"My dad." The boy almost spit the words.

"Tell me. I can help."

But how could she help? The spoken offer of help had come out unbidden, so that must mean she could count on being led to the right way to help.

"I need to know how to help you, and only you can tell me that. First, will you hand me that baby? A baby is no good to you. He can't understand anything. I can. I can listen to you and find out what help you need."

The gun was still wavering. It was undoubtedly very heavy.

"Don't come any closer."

Careful, careful. He's so angry – and so frightened.

"I'm not moving. I won't come closer unless you tell me it's okay."

Carrie didn't look around, but she was aware of silence in the mall. The carols, even the mother's crying, had stopped. All she could hear was her own thumping heart and then, in the background, the easily recognizable creak of a police officer's equipment belt. *No, no, give me time. Let me get the baby away from him. Let me help both of these children.*

The people who walked in darkness have seen a great light. This boy needed that light.

Where was Henry? Still at the car, she hoped.
Before she met him he had been a cop and, finally,
a Police Major. He might feel pushed to intervene.

"Son, let me take the baby and give him to his
mother. I will stay with you instead."

Suddenly the boy laughed, and the anguish in his
laughter brought tears into Carrie's eyes. "Son?" he
shouted. "Not a son! They took my mom. Now I'm
a nobody."

"You sure are somebody. You are God's child,
and God loves and cares for you right now."

*Am I saying the right things? God, help me believe
what I just said.*

Carrie heard another creak from the equipment
belt. "Everyone," she shouted, "do not bother the
boy in Santa's chair. He is in charge now. Leave him
alone."

The boy stood, his arm still around the baby.
"Nobody move!" he shouted.

"Nobody's moving," Carrie said.

Silence.

"May I come closer now? If you give me the baby,
I will hand him to his mother, then I will sit by you.
I promise that. I want to hear your story."

"Not a story. It's true."

He was waving the gun now, possibly pointing it

at first one target behind her, then another but, for the moment he wasn't pointing the gun at the baby. She didn't dare look around but could feel tension vibrating, filling the mall concourse.

"Son, give me the baby. Let his mother take him."

"Mother?" Tears glistened in his eyes. Maybe that was a reason for gratitude. She took a step forward and could see that his eyes were blue. The boy's hair was a dirty blond.

"I am a mother, too. I have a son like you. His name is Rob. Now, why don't you give me that baby so his mother can take him away? You don't need him, I will stay with you." She took a few more sliding steps toward Santa's platform, letting her toes tell her when she had reached the edge.

Moving so quickly that Carrie almost jerked back in fright, the boy shoved the baby into her arms, then pointed the wobbling gun toward her.

She could feel the child moving. He was breathing evenly, and it looked like all that had bled was a small scratch on his face. She decided the spots on his overalls were leftovers from his latest meal. *Another reason to be grateful.*

As she turned toward the child's mother, Carrie glanced up and saw an almost empty mall. Almost. Henry sat alone on their bench, waiting for her. He looked so casual. What was he thinking right now?

Blessed is the Lord our God, Ruler of the universe, who performed wondrous deeds at this season.

The mother reached her arms out to Carrie, took her son, murmured, "Thank you," and hurried away. A woman in uniform came from behind a display in the Outdoor Store and pulled mother and child out of sight.

"Now," Carrie said, "tell me all about it." She sat on the edge of the platform and turned toward the boy. The hole in the gun barrel, so close now, looked huge. The weapon obviously worked. She'd heard two shots. Thank God there had been no more.

Where did this kid get a loaded gun?

Stupid question. Many houses had guns in them. A kid couldn't buy one, even if he had enough money, so this gun had probably been kept in the house where the boy lived, or it was stolen.

Henry still had two revolvers left from his time as a police officer, and they were in her house now. He'd told her some time ago that he had no interest in carrying a gun and always kept his unloaded and locked away. He didn't even have ammunition for them. The last time either of those guns had been fired was during a convenience store robbery several years ago. Though Henry had arrived too late to save the store clerk, he fired quickly to save himself when the robber turned to shoot him. There had been no question that the killing had been justifiable homicide, but Henry himself still couldn't justify it.

"He was just a boy, Carrie, only thirteen."

A boy. Carrie couldn't hold back tears for Henry and the long dead boy.

She turned tear-filled eyes toward the boy who was right here and still alive. "Okay, I'm listening," she said, letting him see her tears.

The gun wavered again, but some of the time it was still pointed at her.

"They...they say I can't live with Mom. I have to go live with my dad and his new family. Just because Mom has it so tough and was trying to help. That old bike had been buried in a garden shed all the years she worked for that family. Doubt they even remembered it was there. Rich folks like that don't need an old bike. They'd-a never known it was missing if an uncle come to visit hadn't gone into the shed to look for some of his old toys. Now Mom's in jail just because of that. We don't have no money for bail."

"Was the bike to be a Christmas present for you?"

"Yeah, kinda. See, someone stole my old bike, and I can't hardly walk my paper route and still make it to school on time. Papers don't come early enough.

"The cops didn't pay but little attention to us about my stolen bike. Huh! They sure paid attention to that rich lady Mom works for, though I think they was a bit surprised when they come for the bike and saw how old it was. We'd looked for bikes at Goodwill and the Sharing Shop, but there wasn't none. All this one needed was newer tires. I could-a painted it later. Red." He stopped talking and looked around the mall, probably not really seeing anything. Then his eyes came back to Carrie.

"Mom said it had been in that shed even before she went to work there. Mom knew about the bike because ever so often the rich lady had her take things to store in the shed."

"Your mom works hard."

"Two jobs. Cleaning and cooking and ironing all day. Waitress at night." He stared at the floor, then lifted his chin and looked into her face. "They told my dad to come get me. He wouldn't-a said yes if the cops didn't ask. He never even gives us money when he's s'posed to." Now his eyes filled with tears.

"Lady, you said you could help. How you gonna do that?"

"Well, we'll see how to undo this mess you and your mom got stuck in. Do you go to church?"

"Mom's too tired now. She works late at the diner on Saturday. Used to go. Lord's Chapel. Nice folks. Gave us food sometimes."

The gun, held loosely in his right hand, was pointing at the floor.

"Then you know about Jesus being born to help us live better lives. So, let's get started doing that. Hand me the gun."

Miraculously, he did.

"Now, hold my hand and we'll stay close together. My husband is over there on that bench, and he knows a lot about how to fix problems like this. Both of us will be with you. We'll talk to people here and then find someone who can help you and your mom."

God, stay with us. Help us say and do the right things. If you can part the Red Sea, you can be with us as we walk with this child. Be with us as we find the right people to understand and help.

Then, with the assistance of an amazing number of people who felt the true Christmas spirit, and because Henry knew how to work well with law enforcement people, that's exactly what happened. The story about the boy and his mother was in the newspapers, then all over the Internet, and brought job offers and many good things to them. But not a bike.

On Christmas Eve, Carrie and Henry sat quietly at home admiring their Christmas tree and the music on TV. There were gifts for family members and friends under their tree, but none for Carrie and Henry. There would be plenty of noise and excitement on the following day, and all those coming to visit would probably bring gifts but, as yet, they had nothing visible there.

A week earlier they had decided they would shop together for a gift the two of them could share. They chose a store called Wheels Alive.

They kept their new red bike only long enough for Carrie to tie a big green bow on the handle bars, and then they drove it to the home of a skinny boy who, yelping with glee, rode it away from Henry's truck without even taking off the bow.

"That kid has a really nice smile," Henry said.

SAVED BY A TRAIN

"Don't stop to talk." Henry took Carrie's arm as they left the church auditorium.

"Just give me a minute to say hello to Eleanor."

"Not now. We have to be someplace by 12:30."

"Huh? Sunday Dinner, I suppose, and since it's Mothers' Day there will be crowds, but I don't mind waiting. Or do we have reservations?"

"I'm not saying, but we need to be someplace by 12:30. Your son's orders, if you must know. Since he's conducting that seminar for his department at the university this weekend he arranged a special treat for you *in absentia*. He wants it to be a complete surprise and made me swear I wouldn't tell you anything about it."

"Oh, well then—how exciting. What is it? I suppose something to do with food since it is time for dinner."

"Did you hear me say 'complete surprise?'"

"Well, he won't know if you tell me."

"Nope."

"A hint then. Anticipation is part of the fun."

"Nope. And he also insisted I have you put this over your head."

"Henry, that's a paper bag."

"I know what a paper bag is, Carrie. But I cut it down so it would just rest, upside down, on your shoulders."

"What? That's loony. I will not put that bag over my head."

"Rob said to insist. He knows you'll peek if I simply tell you to shut your eyes or even put a blindfold on you."

"Oh, all right. And I hope the police stop you, thinking you're kidnapping me or something."

Henry just laughed and headed toward the highway.

The bag made a rattling sound. "Smells funny in here."

"Like a paper bag, I assume. I got a clean one from the grocery store."

They rode in silence for some time, and, try as she might, Carrie could not make sense of their route, though she counted stop lights and turns and tried to picture what they meant.

Then she heard a train whistle. "I assume that's the Arkansas and Missouri train, so we must be somewhere near Arkansas and Missouri tracks. Could be a freight train blowing for a crossing since A&M doesn't usually have excursion rides on Sunday...or... do they? Like maybe on Mothers' Day?"

Henry's exasperated sigh could be heard through the paper bag.

* * *

Carrie was silent for a long time after she and Henry were seated at a bouquet-adorned table for two in the train's dining car. Finally, she said, "I know all these passenger cars are quite old and have been restored by A&M, but it's hard to believe this dining car wasn't manufactured last year or even last month. The white tin ceiling probably could be original, though it's obviously freshly painted. I wouldn't exactly call it beautiful, but it is interesting. Makes me think of one of Shirley's square-patterned quilts, assuming she'd ever make an all-white quilt."

"Uh-huh," Henry said.

There was another silence while Carrie's head swiveled back and forth. Finally she asked, "Do you know what kind of wood was used in here? Is it really old? If so, they did a beautiful job of refinishing and polishing all the curves and carvings. The lighting fixtures look antique, but I bet they aren't. They're too perfect. Not even a chip or scratch. I am impressed. Feel free to report that fact to my son."

"Uh-huh," Henry said.

After a server brought their drink orders and Henry had poked at his phone, Carrie leaned back in her chair and closed her eyes. "It even smells interesting, like...like..."

"Like lunch," Henry said, as decoratively arranged plates of food were put in front of them, conversation ended, and chewing began.

* * *

Finally Carrie said, "That was the most elegant chicken salad I've ever tasted. Hated to mess it up though, since everything on the plate was arranged like a work of art. Do you think things taste better when they're arranged like this was?"

"Plop on a plate is good enough for me—assuming one of us has cooked, of course."

She laughed, then said, "I guess I should do more cooking. Are you sorry you didn't marry a gourmet cook, Henry?"

"Nope. You didn't marry one either. We both knew what we were getting before we said 'I do.' And, now that we have that settled, let's just enjoy the ride your son is paying for."

"Um hm. I am enjoying it.

"Henry, have you been able to identify where we

are when we go through towns we drive in regularly? From the back side, everything looks anonymous."

"Yes, it does, but I haven't been thinking about that or paying attention to whether or not I could identify a place. It is interesting to view buildings from a new angle, whether we know what they are or not. I guess retail stores and business buildings only need to offer enough identification in back to guide delivery trucks and trash collectors, and not the general public. Think about it. What if you saw a trash container labeled, say, J. C. Penney, and thought only 'what an ugly mess?' Better to remain anonymous rather than advertise who owns an ugly, over-full trash container."

"Not all trash containers are ugly. There was one back there that had sunflowers painted all over it. Didn't you see it?"

"Missed that. But have you noticed the train slowing down? It started doing that several minutes ago."

"Oh, I feel it now. Maybe the train is stopping because something interesting is planned to entertain us. Do you already know what it is? Are we going to a street fair or to watch a fake train robbery? Railway people have acted out train robberies before. I saw one at the Van Buren Station on National Train Day.

Doesn't seem very appropriate for Mothers' Day, though."

Henry leaned forward to look out the window. "They said nothing about anything happening outside the train when I picked up our tickets."

The conductor appeared at the front of their car. "Sorry folks, but we're having to stop. We got word from our dispatcher a while ago that there's some kind of celebration going on in the park here and festivities have spilled over into the street. There's a worry that people, without thinking, might get too close to the tracks. We want to be sure they're cleared safely away before we move on. While we're taking care of this, if you'd like more coffee or pop, the servers will be glad to get it for you. It's okay to stand and stretch, but please stay in this car."

Carrie stood and went to a window across the aisle. "Oh, I see what's going on. It's a wedding celebration. Easy to tell because of the bride's white gown. The people look mostly Mexican, or maybe I should say Hispanic, but some are Caucasian. The bride has blond hair. What fun it will be to watch their celebration for a while. A couple of the conductors from the other cars are out there now, talking to folks."

She laughed. "I think some of the participants

have had too much to drink. Two of the men are trying to dance and are only managing to be funny. I don't see anyone playing music, though. And I know right where we are now. There's the Caboose Café. We've eaten there."

Carrie returned to their side of the aisle and leaned past Henry, who had shut his eyes, letting the unexpected break pull him into drowsiness.

"Not much going on over here," she said. "Everyone is on the other side of the tracks and...Oh! OH! Henry, look. There's a man—NO! He has a gun."

Henry had retained a law officer's ability to be instantly alert, and his head joined Carrie's at the window.

"Where? I don't see anyone."

"He's running toward the back of the train now. It sure wasn't a handgun." She reached for her phone. "I'm calling 911."

Since her words had been almost shouted, quiet conversation in the car stopped at once, and a woman's voice screeched into the silence, "I saw him, he has a big gun." She dropped to the floor with another shriek, taking a tablecloth, glassware, and a vase of flowers with her. After only a few seconds, several other passengers followed her down, though some stayed at their windows, either uncertain about what to do, or wanting to keep an eye on any pending activity.

The conductor, who had been seated at the front of the car, was standing again. "Everyone get away from the windows. Looks like our train has stopped between the gunman and the crowd on the other side. I don't know what's going on, but I've locked the doors, and we've called 911 for help."

Carrie said, "He's wearing a green jacket."

Staccato conversation burst out. Above the clamor a male voice asked, "Anyone know if the sides of this car are bullet-proof? I think we should move into the aisle."

Ducking, Carrie went back across the aisle, knelt, and looked over the windowsill. "People are scattering now, running every which way. But I don't see the man in the green jacket. Oh, dear God, there he is, coming from the back of the train. He's ignoring the men who were trying to dance and has lifted the gun. He's pointing it toward the bride and groom."

Please, please, God, oh, please, keep everyone safe. Please help all of them be safe. Stop the man with the gun. She shut her eyes.

Henry knelt beside her, stayed there in silence for a few minutes, then said, "It's okay to look now, my dear. We've seen a sort of miracle. Those two dancing men fell on the back of the shooter, and their momentum knocked him flat on his face. Their combined weight is holding him down. One of the other men yanked the gun away from him, and three police cars have arrived."

Carrie lifted her head and looked, then started to giggle, sounding like she was on the edge of hysterics. "Well, maybe the guy with the gun wanted to be the one who married that woman. If he did, he sure had a heck of a way to show it."

The train began moving forward again, very slowly. It cleared the street, then stopped, and two police officers came into their car to begin interviews. Outside, officers were organizing wedding guests into groups for interviews. Servers came from the Caboose Café carrying trays of cheese and crackers, while some of the wedding guests followed, bringing everyone in the train tiny bits of wedding cake wrapped in napkins that read "Eloise and Hector."

Eloise and Hector, however, had disappeared. Carrie, after collecting her tumbling thoughts into some reasonable order, stayed at the window and saw the bride and groom, unnoticed, get into what was probably a hired limousine, thus separating themselves from activity that now seemed like a celebration—as it really should be, she decided, considering what might have happened.

After she told a police officer what she had seen and noticed that Henry was talking cop-language with one of the other officers, she left the dining car and strolled casually over to the front door of the limousine, opened it, stepped up, and perched her behind on a front seat. She leaned over to look at a crying bride and frowning groom. He was stroking his bride's hand and saying, "Ellie, Ellie, it's okay, it's okay," in clear English with a slight Spanish accent.

"He's right. It is okay now," Carrie said to the bride, "and no one was hurt."

"But that was my brother Eddie. He was going to kill us because he thinks I should marry one of my own 'kind,'" the bride said, unleashing a new torrent of tears.

"Well, yes, maybe he thought he was, but now he has an open path toward learning several ideas that are very important, if he will pay attention to them. I suppose he'll go to prison for a time, but God was with us all, including your brother. He has been saved from committing a terrible act, and now he can make changes in his thinking and in his life.

"I bet this event will be all over the Internet within minutes, and it will probably appear in newspapers as well. Others will have a chance to think more broadly and maybe learn lessons. Marriages like yours will undoubtedly increase in the future. More of us need to see that as entirely normal."

The bride snuffled and took the handkerchief Hector handed her.

Carrie thought a moment, then continued, "Consider yourselves part of a crusade. Love can span races, tribes, and cultures throughout all humanity. Because of what happened here, your story will spread, maybe even worldwide. And, of course, your brother will have access to the help he needs to heal his mental problems and prejudices.

"You know what I think? I think you can help Eddie by staying in touch with him." She looked directly at Hector. "As a couple."

He smiled, very slightly, and nodded.

"Maybe," she said, "if you have a son someday, you might even want to name him Edward and call him Little Eddie."

After a silence, Eloise blew her nose, turned to Hector, and said, "I'm okay now. We're both okay, and we're together. Thank you, Miss...whoever you are. Our angel."

Carrie smiled at them, slid out of her seat, shut

the door as quietly as she could, and went to join Henry.

WHATEVER HAPPENED TO DANA JEAN?

Carrie stopped at the edge of the garden, watched her husband put a ripe tomato in his basket, then said, "S'posed to stay in the 80s today, and it still feels pleasant, so Shirley and I are going berry picking. I noticed the blackberries on the vines along the road have begun to turn black, and she says she'd enjoy the break from tending to cows, and the walk with me, though they do have blackberry bushes on their farm. I'm meeting her at the head of our lane."

Henry straightened up and said, "Stay on the road. Chiggers and ticks are pretty heavy right now."

"Too right! I did spray my clothes, and we'll be careful. See you in an hour or so."

Shirley was waiting when Carrie reached the road. She was dressed like Carrie in tall boots, jeans, a long-sleeved shirt, and a wide-brimmed hat. "Think one of those lady fashion magazines would do somethin' about how to dress for summer berry picking?" she said. "Only thing is, truth be told, you're not skinny enough for them. Remember?"

Carrie laughed and nodded. When she married Amos, her first husband, a plain suit had been appropriate for the judge's office. For her much dressier wedding to Henry, she had wanted a real wedding dress, and, at her insistence, she and Shirley looked at dozens of photos in the bridal magazines Carrie brought home from the grocery store. When Shirley dropped the last magazine on the floor, she said, "Dresses look like they're only fit for putting over a broomstick with bazooms. So, will you listen to me now? I will make your wedding dress. Made both my girls' dresses, I can easy make yours."

Carrie, who'd felt an increasing despair after studying photo after photo of thin young brides with—as Shirley had noted—bazooms coming out of low-cut dress tops, had accepted the offer. Shirley was, therefore, quite familiar with every curve in Carrie's body.

As they moved along the road, picking berries from bushes leaning over pasture fences, Shirley pointed at pairs of bushes and said, "This here's my bush, and that's yours. We don't want to run into each other and get scratched. Careful the barbed wire, it's worse than berry thorns."

Carrie always nodded agreement, but rarely spoke, since she usually had a mouth full of berries.

After they had gone about a half mile along the road, Shirley turned toward a partly overgrown dirt road angling off into a farm that, Carrie knew, had been abandoned for many years. "Let's try our luck down that old road. Besides, I'm curious to see if Floyd Jackson's old Dodge truck is still there."

"Ah, the Jackson farm," Carrie said. "When Amos and I were looking at Ozarks property, oh, probably ten years before Amos was killed and I moved here to our land, we were told about the Jackson farm, but the real estate agent said it wouldn't be a good buy. Never said why, but by then we had seen the land that became Blackberry Hollow and liked the fact that the land had a live spring and a creek. We never looked at this place. Odd that it's never sold."

"Not so odd. It's not 'zactly haunted, but bad things happened here. Besides, there might be a living Jackson heir somewhere. There was a daughter, Dana Jean, though folks say she's prob'ly dead. They say Floyd Jackson killed her, though her body was never found.

"No question but what he did kill his wife. There was a big deal trial, and he went to prison. He died there just a few months ago. Dana Jean disappeared about the same time her mother died, so guess that's why the talk is he killed her too."

"How awful. How old was she?"

"Sixteen or seventeen, as I recall."

"Did she have a boyfriend?"

"I never heard of one. But her daddy would have stopped that anyway. He was always an angry man, a drinker, and had fits of rage. Wanted to control his women, and everything else, I reckon. Roger said the men talking at the café in town didn't like him much, worried he'd fly off in a rage at one of them if they weren't careful about what they said. Ended up beating his wife to death, so folks still think he did that to the daughter, too, and somehow got rid of her body, carrying it off somewhere before he killed his wife. They looked for new digging in the woods and searched other places, but never found anything. In these hills and hollows though—who knows?"

"Oh, Shirley."

"Sheriff did say the wife was made unconscious quick from a hit on her head, though she was almost unrecognizable when they found her. Guess he just kept on beating until his rage wore off."

"Not sure I want to go down there."

"That was at least fifteen years ago. I'm sure the place is cleaned of evil by now. Growing plants and trees tend to do that, at least for me. It used to be a pretty place, thanks to Leona Jackson." Shirley had already started down the road, so Carrie followed, trying to erase an image of Leona Jackson.

"I hope the daughter is alive and happy somewhere."

"We all do. Since Floyd Jackson is dead now, mebee she'll come back to claim her land, at least if she hears he's gone. I've always hoped he didn't kill her and she just ran away."

"Wonder why she didn't leave earlier."

"Stayed around because of her mother, I reckon."

"Um. Yes, I see."

Carrie noticed that Shirley was ignoring the berry bushes they passed, and she followed along, hesitating only to pick a few to put in her mouth since she knew they could pick when they came back this way.

"Well, I'll be, Floyd Jackson's old red truck is still here. I did wonder if somebody hadn't hauled it away by now to sell for scrap. Prob'ly could do it without anyone noticing, especially at night." Shirley started toward the truck, wading through weedy undergrowth and a waist-high tangle of Queen Anne's lace.

Carrie stayed on the road, staring at the truck, now largely buried in honeysuckle vines and surrounded by white flower heads. The truck's front was still visible, though most of the red paint was more rust color than red. It looked like the windshield glass was still intact.

"Someone's been here," Shirley said. "They opened the truck door, and it swept away the vines. Looks like the stem breaks are pretty fresh."

Hinges shrieked as she, also, opened the door. After a long silence, Shirley said, "Come here, Carrie."

"Uh, can't you just tell me about it? I'm not eager to get into that heavy growth. Both chiggers and ticks are especially fond of me."

"Well, suit yourself, but I think I need a witness to what I see here. You got your phone that takes pictures with you?"

"Yes."

"Okay, you need to make a picture here."

Now Carrie forgot about biting pests and pushed through the tangle toward Shirley, who shoved the squawking door open a few more inches and said, "Look there."

The photo of a man was stuck to the back of the partly missing cover on the driver's seat. A small kitchen knife held it in place.

"Floyd Jackson?" Carrie asked.

"Yup. Take your picture."

"Okay." Carrie leaned against the seat edge and took several pictures, including one straight on, showing the man's face clearly. Then she backed away from the truck and said, "Now, shouldn't we get out of here?"

"No, I gotta walk on to the house. Bet someone's been there, too. You can leave if you want, but it's not much further." Shirley banged the truck door shut, and the two of them returned to the road. Unwilling to leave her friend alone, Carrie followed Shirley along the road, and, in a short while they rounded a curve, and came into an overgrown yard surrounding a native stone house. Tracks in the weeds showed some vehicle had been there many times. An outhouse with a missing roof was visible behind the house.

Cicadas and a few bird calls were all that broke the silence as they approached the house's front porch and Shirley stepped on the large flat stone that led to the porch floor. "I wonder if the door is locked."

"Shirley, I'm not going in there, and I don't think you should either. From these tire tracks, it looks like someone may be staying here or at least visiting."

Shirley leaned over the porch rail, which creaked but held, and said, "Yup, could be. And look here. Someone's been weeding Leona's flowerbed. The iris is still going strong, and someone's begun to clear around it. They even left a trowel here on the edge of the porch."

"All the more reason to get out of here. We are trespassing. Let's leave." Carrie turned away and began a fast walk back along the old road, leaving Shirley standing, statue still, on the porch.

Before she started around the road's curve she turned back and shouted, "Come on. I'm going back to the main road, and I don't feel good about leaving you here alone."

As Carrie took a few more steps it was a relief to hear small road rocks skittering under Shirley's boots as she hurried away from the house. "Place just now gave me a chill," she said when she reached Carrie's side. "No more we can do here today, but somebody oughta check this out. Mebee we can come back with Henry and Roger, or can get the sheriff to come."

"Maybe," Carrie said.

"Do you think Henry would take your pictures to the sheriff's deputy he knows?"

"I'll ask," Carrie said, though she was pretty sure the photo wasn't going to raise enough interest to invite a visit to a place that had been abandoned for many years. Could even be kids up to mischief, though weeding a flowerbed didn't seem to fit that.

When they reached the lane to Blackberry Hollow, Shirley said, "I should go along home and start lunch for Roger and Junior. Let me know what Henry says. Sorry about the berry picking. Guess you can go out again tomorrow."

Carrie nodded and hurried home to Henry.

* * *

At Carrie's urging, Henry did call the Sheriff's Department to report what Carrie and Shirley had found at the old Jackson place, but he got only what he'd told Carrie would be the probable response.

"You say they saw no one there and the place is privately owned?" the deputy asked Henry. "Not much we can do. I've heard about the murder of Leona Jackson, a big thing in this usually quiet county, and I can't say as I blame anyone who'd put a knife through his photo, though that's off the record, of course."

* * *

Forgoing the promised dish of fresh blackberries until later in the evening, Henry suggested they go into town for an early supper at Taco Mama's. They were escorted to a booth by a server Carrie didn't recognize, and she studied the woman's face as she put their basket of chips and cups of salsa on the table. When they had finished ordering, Carrie spoke quickly as the woman began to turn away. "Are you taking Goldie's place? Did her baby come?"

The woman's surprise was evident. After a pause, she finally said, "No, not yet, but the doctor told her it could be any time now. She's on maternity leave."

"Sorry to have surprised you with a personal question. My husband and I eat at Taco Mama's quite often, so we've gotten to know many of the people who work here. Guess I'd better introduce myself. I'm Carrie, and he's Henry. You must have come on staff after our last visit. Are you working the same shift that Goldie did?"

The woman said, "Yes, and I've been here almost a month now. My name is Donna. Anyway, welcome to Taco Mama's."

As the woman walked away, then stopped to clear dishes from a table next to them, Carrie leaned toward Henry and continued what had become an ongoing conversation about Dana Jean Jackson. "Suppose Dana Jean is still alive. What could happen next? Let's assume she hears some way—wherever she is now—that her father has died in prison. Would she come home?"

Henry said nothing until after the server headed toward the kitchen with her stack of dirty plates, then, very quietly, he spoke. "Interesting. Our server nearly dropped a glass a moment ago. I think it was when she heard you say the name Dana Jean."

"Oh, my. Do you think she knew the girl or...or maybe...is the girl? Wooo!"

"Unlikely she is the girl—or woman—now. Wouldn't some people here recognize her, even so many years later?"

"According to Shirley, doubtful. At first she was home schooled, though she did go to high school here, but Shirley says her dad always brought her and picked her up immediately after school. She never got out into the community and, so far as Shirley knows, had no close friends here. But this woman does look to be about the right age."

When she saw the server returning with their order, Carrie immediately turned to Henry and, as if she was in the middle of a conversation, said, "I think Goldie said she was going to name their little girl Dana something-or-other. Was it Jane? She had heard the name and liked it. I sure am looking forward to seeing that baby and—oh, thank you, Donna. This looks delicious."

Henry chuckled. "I paid no attention to any talk about names. But for now, let's eat. I'm hungry, and seeing this makes me even hungrier. It does look wonderful."

"You folks need anything more now?"

"Nope, we're fine."

"I'll check with you about dessert later."

Perhaps hoping to hear more of their conversation, the woman then sat in a nearby booth and began rolling tableware in napkins, but Henry and Carrie were too busy eating to talk. Before they finished, the regular evening supper rush began, claiming all of Donna's time.

Finally Carrie put down her fork and said, "You don't want dessert. We have blackberries at home. I put some in two bowls and sprinkled just a tiny bit of sugar over them. They're in the refrigerator waiting for two spoons."

* * *

The next morning Henry was working at their wood pile using the motorized log splitter when Carrie appeared, dressed once more in her berry-picking clothes. She watched the splitter for a couple of minutes, then said, "That thing always fascinates me. When it closes on the end of a piece of wood it seems to be thinking for a minute. Then all of a sudden, the log responds to the wedge's pressure and, pop, you've got two pieces."

"Yep, and it sure beats whacking logs apart with an ax. I approve of these modern inventions." He turned off the splitter and asked, "You going berry picking again?"

"Yes, still a lot of them available. And I thought I'd walk along the old road to the Jackson's and see what I can find there."

"Now, Carrie..."

"Well, I assume Donna, or Dana Jean, wouldn't leave for work at Taco Mama's until around 10:00, so she could be at the Jackson house right now. I wanted to get the message to her that people here will be very glad to see her. Don't know if I'll say anything about the general worry that her dad killed her, though."

Henry took off his gloves. "Carrie, it's not wise for you to go there. Leave the Jackson place and what you suspect alone, at least for a while. Besides, you'd be trespassing. It might not be safe."

"That sounds a bit like your 'stay out of danger' cop talk."

"It is. If Donna realizes we suspect who she is, and, if she doesn't want to be outed, she could even be dangerous. What if she inherited Floyd Jackson's temper?"

"All I want to do is let her know this community will welcome her home. I'd be going there as a friend."

"Think! For one thing, we aren't at all sure she is Dana Jean. Two, how can you know 100% that all will welcome her? And, I might add, you shouldn't jump in the middle of something that really does not concern you. Think about the photo stabbed into the seat back of the truck. That action depicts something close to rage. And, think about this, too. It might not have been Dana Jean Jackson who did it."

"Oh, come on. That seems unlikely to me. Who else would have done it? Besides, she may just be back home to claim her property, found the truck still here, and used it as an outlet for remembered feelings. Could you blame her?"

"Then there wouldn't be much reason for secrecy, would there? That's just one of many things you—we—don't know concerning the reason Dana Jean Jackson may be back home. Maybe she wants to stay unidentified until she solves some issue that we know nothing about."

"Well..."

"You get results when you pray. Go back in the house and approach this that way."

"Okay, but I do want to get more berries first."

"I'll pick with you; we can get twice as many."

She laughed, "Uh-huh, and you can be sure I don't visit Dana Jean Jackson. Well, come on then."

They picked in silence, and Carrie was pleased to see that Henry ate about as many as she did, though a coating of dust on those nearest the road was somewhat off-putting. "See, we should have gone along the Jackson road, no dust there."

He blew on a berry and popped it in his mouth. "I'm doing okay."

She leaned over to look in his bucket. "Well, I'd say you are. From now on, you can do our berry picking, you've got about twice as many as I do. What's your secret?"

"My hands are bigger than yours. I can pull off several at once."

Just then they both heard the sound of an approaching vehicle, and she said, "You may want to cover your nose and mouth. More dust coming."

The car slowed to a crawl behind them and, grateful for the consideration, Carrie turned to wave a thanks. The driver was Donna/Dana Jackson, and she faced ahead, ignoring the wave.

"Ah, well, guess it's safe to go down Jackson Road now. Look who's driving that car."

"I see, but there are still plenty of berries here."

They continued on down the main road, and, in just a few minutes, car and driver returned and, as Carrie watched, turned in at the Jackson road.

"Now will you believe she does not want us meddling in her affairs?" Henry said.

"Could be she forgot something."

"Keep picking. We'll see if she comes back out. Looks like she is staying in the old Jackson house, and she won't have to leave for work for another forty-five minutes."

In about thirty minutes Henry said, "My bucket is almost full. Let's go home. I assume you planned to make a berry pie with that crust in the refrigerator? Of course, I could do it, but I want to finish log splitting today. Okay?"

"I'm on it. Shower, then pie. Won't be cool enough for you to taste when you come in, but that's okay. I don't mind if you take bites and the juice runs down your chin. See you noonish."

When Henry came in the kitchen at noon, Carrie said, "I called Shirley and told her about this morning. She said she'll get Roger to start a conversation in town when he goes in for coffee after milking in the morning. Maybe, if there is something more to the Jackson story, he can find out, even if it's only gossip."

"I wish you'd just drop this whole Jackson issue. Yes, she may be Dana Jean Jackson. But isn't it obvious she's not ready to reveal who she is? She is probably worried now that you'll expose her identity before she is ready to reveal it herself. I hope Roger doesn't blow her cover in town."

"He won't. Shirley and I talked about that. But I thought of something else. If she does really want to hide her identity, do you think she'll leave here since, as you say, she probably realizes we have figured out who she is? I wish I'd kept my mouth shut about the name Dana. It would seem pretty crazy if we ate at Taco Mama's again this evening. But, if we did, I could make a point of calling her Donna and otherwise ignore her."

"Come on, Carrie. I'm sure the woman is not stupid. Don't you think she'd be double spooked if you did that?"

He spooned up another bite of pie, chewed and swallowed, then said, "Drop it, drop it, drop it! No more conversation about anything Jackson.

"By the way, this sure is good pie, and, look here, I've eaten at least a quarter of it and spooned up all the extra juice. Would you like me to put some in a bowl for you?"

* * *

Shirley phoned the next afternoon to say she and Roger would like to come up to discuss this 'Jackson thing.'

"You don't hafta fix anything, I just made oatmeal cookies with raisins. I know that's your favorite, and

I don't think Henry exactly hates them. I'll bring along enough for the four of us. You can fix the coffee."

"Great. Thank you. You coming now?"

"Yup."

Carrie called the news to Henry, who was in his chair reading the morning paper, and went to the kitchen to put on the kettle. She had never decided if Shirley and Roger simply tolerated her instant coffee, or actually thought it was good, but, even on their introduction to it the first time they visited Blackberry Hollow almost three years ago, neither she nor Roger had said anything. However, the Booths, as well as their other friends in the area, always perked.

When the four of them were seated at the break-fast room table with cups and cookie plates, Roger said, "All the regulars were there this morning, and it's always easy to start a conversation about Floyd Jackson and his family. After a bit of talk about what happened back then, Bert Goodings spoke up, asking if we knew anything about any more Jackson kids. O'course none of us had ever heard about anyone but Dana Jean, so we all said no, and Bert took off with his story. Seems Dana Jean was at the road waiting for the mail when she was about—oh, maybe eight or ten—and she was crying and said her daddy was trying to drown the baby. Bert said the mail deliverer assumed it was a baby kitten or puppy that Floyd wouldn't tolerate, and he told her to take the baby over to the neighbors and leave it on their porch. He never heard no more, though she still did come up for the mail sometimes.

"So, I was wondering, do you suppose there really could have been a human baby she was talking about?"

"Doesn't seem likely," Carrie said. "Oh, my goodness, how awful to think about that. And, if it was a human baby, what happened to it? Surely neighbors would have said something if a baby was left on their porch. Wouldn't they have raised an alarm? But, if there was a real baby, maybe that has something to do with why she's not revealing her identity. There could be something to settle there. Henry, I'm not sure that keeping quiet about our guess that she's Dana Jean Jackson is the best idea now. She could be in a real mental tangle and need understanding friends. What if she thinks that her sibling is still alive, and that person, not she, might be the one to inherit the old homestead, especially if it's a male."

Henry said, "I don't know that the law today would say a male had to inherit unless there was a will saying so, and it doesn't seem likely that Floyd Jackson ever wrote a will of any kind."

Shirley said, "Roger, why don't we go into town now and see if we can get a chat with Chester Blevins. He might be able to advise us on the law."

* * *

Armed with new information, and with Henry content to only advise caution, the four of them walked down the road to the Jackson home the next morning. The same car Carrie and Henry had seen leaving the day before was parked next to the house.

Shirley stepped up on the porch and knocked. At first Carrie thought no one was going to answer, but then a man dressed in overalls opened the door and stood there grinning at them. Finally he said, "Hu'lo, I'm Donnie, who are you?"

For a moment, no one said anything more, but Roger recovered first, and said, "Good morning, Donnie. I'm your neighbor. My name is Roger, and this here's my wife, Shirley. Yonder are our friends, Carrie and Henry."

The young man shifted from one foot to another, then wiped a hand on his overalls and stuck it out toward Roger, who took it for an awkward shake as both of them smiled, and Donnie said, "Pleased to make your—to meet you. Are you Dana's friends?

She didn't hear you knock, she's in the kitchen."

"Yes, we're her friends," Carrie said. "Can she come and say hello?"

The man turned without responding, disappeared, and, in a minute, Donna/Dana appeared. Donnie Jackson was not with her.

"Oh," she said. "Oh."

"We've come as neighbors and friends," Roger said. "We're Roger and Shirley Booth. These folks here, Carrie and Henry, figured out who you must be, and we're here to welcome you and your brother back home and to see if there is any way we can help you with, well, with anything you need help with."

She looked around. "We don't have much furniture, so I can't ask you in to sit down. Donnie and I have been sleeping on mattresses on the floor. I don't know about how you could help us, though we sure need it. I've been trying to figure out how to straighten out legal questions about Donnie and me before I told anyone who I was. I figured we did still own this place, one of us at least, so we could stay here, though there isn't any electricity or running water yet. I do have a camping stove and propane and some lanterns, and I've been buying big bottles of water to wash with and drink. Since I got the job at the restaurant they sometimes let me bring left-over food home. That's a big help."

"How long have you been here?" Henry asked.

"A couple of months now. How did you figure out who we are?"

"Well," Shirley said, "that photo of your dad stuck to the seat on the old truck started it. And Carrie and Henry here noticed how you reacted to the name Dana Jean at Taco Mama's."

"Oh, the photo. Donnie did that when we first came here. He, well, he remembers our dad and what he saw him do, especially when—well, Donnie didn't understand—but he saw Dad on top of me messing around, and me crying. I should have taken the picture down but, well, I—I couldn't bring myself to even touch it."

She was quiet, staring at the floor, but then lifted her head and said, "Donnie is quite special. He's usually very gentle and kind. In fact, that's the first angry thing I've ever seen him do. But when he saw the picture here in the house, he remembered Daddy hurting me, and...and...all the rest, while he watched. He was just a little boy then, but he remembered."

"We understand about the photo; we've heard some of your history." Shirley said. "How about this? Roger can come up about eight o'clock in the morning and take you down to our house for a big breakfast, and he can bring you back in time to get your car and go to work. Bring your things, and you and Donnie can shower there, too. And, if you want, you can use my washing machine. Besides that, we have a friend in town who's a lawyer, and he was around when, well, he remembers when your dad's trial was going on, so he knows some details. Maybe he can come to breakfast too and give you some free advice. Okay?"

Dana stared at Shirley in silence for what seemed like a full minute, then she said, "Oh, we'd be so appreciative. Yes, okay. I'd cry now, but I don't dare. It would upset Donnie. I do have papers about his release to me from the state home he was in when I found him, but I don't have any other legal documents. He was born in this house. Mama had only me here to help her, and I don't guess there was ever a birth certificate. Daddy figured out before Donnie was very old that he was, well, special, and he never wanted anyone to know about him. He blamed Mama, but he did hit her around a lot when she was big with Donnie. And then he tried to...in the stock tank, to..." She fell silent, shut her eyes, and bowed her head, shaking it from side to side.

"Never you mind now, we know some of that,"

Shirley said, "but we can all work together and get things straightened out."

Just then Donnie ambled in, eating an apple.

"Oh, Donnie," his sister said, "these nice folks have invited us to have breakfast at their house in the morning, and you can take a shower there."

Donnie took a bite of apple, thought a minute, then asked, "Do you have hot water?"

FOUR-YEAR-OLDS SOLVE A CRIME

A version of this story was originally published by the Rogers, Arkansas, Public Library

* * *

"JEREMY! JEMIMA! HALT! NOW!"

Carrie had already spread her arms to corral two four-year-olds dashing toward parking lot traffic, but Eleanor's ear-breaking shriek served the purpose admirably. It also stopped several pedestrians in their tracks, as well as two cars with their windows down.

There were other cars still looking for parking spaces in the crowded library lot, but they had windows closed to preserve air conditioning. Their drivers only glanced out briefly, perhaps thinking they had imagined hearing a peculiar noise.

Oblivious to the effect her halt order had in the general area, Eleanor grabbed one grandchild's overall strap in each hand and said to her friend, "I'm sorry, but the JJs have been wild ever since I told them we were coming to see Noddy Clown. As you can tell, I should have taken them for a ten-mile run instead, but they do love the Noddy books, and I promised Patricia I'd make sure they *experienced* cultural activities during their summer visit to Nana and Popi."

Eleanor's words began coming in puffs as she galloped toward the library door, towed by two blond, angel-curled children. "What on earth is a cultural experience for a four-year-old?" she gasped. "Experience is the actual word Pat used. I hope a library program"—she paused to breathe—"qualifies. Otherwise I'm not sure what cultural activity for these two is supposed to be."

Eleanor's attempt at conversation ended as the JJs jumped the curb, then came up against the crowd moving slowly toward the library's doors. Stopped cold, the twins began hopping from one foot to the other, which drew the attention of other children in the crowd who began mimicking the action.

"Want a Noddy suit," Jemima said, timing each word to match a hop.

"Next Halloween," Eleanor told her absent-mindedly as she looked back to be sure Carrie was keeping up.

"Noddy suit, Noddy suit," contributed Jeremy, hopping in sync with his twin.

"Stop that kids. I'm not letting go of your straps,

and if you keep jumping you'll rip them. Remember, you begged Nana to buy overalls for you. Well, no more new clothes if you tear these."

The hopping stopped, and both children stared up at their grandmother, eyes preparing to spill tears. Eleanor planted a kiss on top of each head and crooned, "Good for you. This is how we act in crowds."

Her voice went back to adult mode. "Anyway, Carrie, when Patricia was four, things were simpler. I'm sure it was the same for you when Rob was little. We went to the library all the time, but back then I didn't think of it as a cultural experience. I just hope my daughter thinks it was. I'll have to ask her when she calls tonight. Or, maybe I won't. For all I know, she'll say it wasn't cultural and want me to take these two to an art museum, a children's stage play, or even a concert. I shudder to think...

"Hold it, Jeremy, you're about to pull Nana over on her face. We have to wait in line. Remember what Noddy's song says, '*Line up to see the spesh-e-al-a-tee.*'"Eleanor sang the line, and more than one giggle erupted from the crowd.

"Here, Carrie, hang on to him while I manage Jemima." Eleanor hooked Jeremy's overall strap over Carrie's fingers as the crowd pushed through the doors, surged into the central concourse, and, as one, turned right toward the doors to the Children's Library.

They were immediately enclosed in a gaggle of adults, all trying to contain knee-high clown worshippers. A woman in a clown suit and red yarn wig stood in the entrance, greeting children and helping guide the crowd. The badge pinned on her neck ruffle read *Megan Bradley, Children's Librarian.*

Carrie thought, *Megan, I salute you,* as she looked down at the top of Jeremy's head and then surveyed the rest of the children swirling though the double doors.

She was brought back to attention when Jeremy asked, "Where's Noddy?"

Carrie looked down again. The only thing in the boy's field of vision was a very broad area of plaid-covered female backside.

"Up ahead; we're almost there, love."

They finally made it to the carpeted preschool area where children were being seated. A row of toilet plungers linked by heavy yarn outlined a stage area in front, and volunteers dressed in clown regalia guided children to seats. When the twins were safely deposited on a red patch of fluffy carpet, Eleanor and Carrie backed off toward the adult seating area.

"Thanks so much for coming along," Eleanor said. "I'd have had real trouble managing both of them at this level of excitement without your help. Your reward is to enjoy the quiet part of the library in peace—for a while, at least. The clown show is supposed to last an hour. You'll probably know when we're ready to go by the increased noise level. See you then? How about meeting near the desk where you get library cards?"

Carrie smiled at her friend. "Okay. Have fun. You and the twins can tell me all about it on the way home."

"Oh, the kids will do that, never fear."

With a small wave and one last look at the undulating mass of small bodies, Carrie turned toward the concourse. She started laughing as soon as she was out of the Children's Library because Eleanor's two, who would be perfect models for cherubs otherwise, were busy picking their noses and comparing the contents.

Kids! Oh, well. And Eleanor was right. She would enjoy an hour alone in the quiet part of the library.

* * *

Carrie immediately felt immersed in an atmosphere that—as a former research librarian in Tulsa, Oklahoma—she knew and cherished. Libraries were cozy places, offering warmth so palpable she could almost hug it around her. This was true whether she was in a grand new building like this one, or the cinder block library in the small Ozarks town near where she lived. Maybe it was warmth generated by books sharing ideas, knowledge, and entertainment.

She walked along the concourse toward the adult non-fiction section. As she passed the restroom alcove, there was a door whoosh and Noddy Clown, dressed in his trademark red, white, and blue suit and red-and-white face paint, hurried past, almost colliding with her. The tote bag he carried swung around and socked her in the side, but Noddy seemed not to notice. He didn't even say, "S'cuse me," a term insisted on throughout Noddy stories and songs.

He—but this Noddy was not a he. The clown's hurried exit from the women's restroom had proved Noddy to be a SHE.

Hmmm. But then, it wouldn't really matter. In a loose clown suit and, presuming the voice didn't give things away, little kids wouldn't know the difference. Noddy's secret was safe, or at least it was safe with Carrie. However, she would tell Eleanor her gen-u-ine Noddy secret when Jeremy and Jemima weren't around.

After she reached the adult section, Carrie strolled along, reading titles, sometimes removing a book to leaf through pages. When a librarian asked if she needed help, she said, on impulse, "Do you have any adult books about clowns?"

Smiling, he said, "Yes, but most are checked out right now since, as you may perchance have noticed, one of our summer programs in the Children's Library is called 'Clowning Around.'" He led her to a shelf holding books on entertainment and pointed. "There we are, a couple left for you to look at."

Carrie took down both books, found a comfortable chair in a windowed alcove, and sat.

She read about clown make-up (no two faces should be alike), about clown songs, pocket magic (how to put a marble in your pocket and then find it in your mouth), and clown dances, which seemed to consist of a lot of bouncing. She wondered, briefly, if she could entertain the JJs by dressing up like a clown and doing some of this stuff. But, when she tried the movements necessary for getting a marble moved from pocket to mouth, she realized clown tricks were not as easy as the books said. She already knew the dancing wasn't. Ah, well, maybe she and the JJs could write a clown song.

'Noddy-Noddy, give a little laughy

Noddy-laughy fall down with a flappy.'

She laughed aloud as the words flashed through her thoughts, then covered her mouth with her hand when a bearded man dressed in cargo shorts and a t-shirt proclaiming *"Who Cares!"* looked up from his sports magazine and scowled.

Carrie wanted to say, "Well, you aren't so stuffed-shirt-conventional-looking yourself," but, of course, she didn't. This was, after all, a library, and her years in Tulsa's Central Library had taught her what would be appropriate here. She did grin at *"Who Cares!"* but he returned to his magazine without responding.

Humpf. Well, phooey on him. She imagined leaping out of her chair and doing a floppy-limbed dance while singing her song to the bearded man. Then she'd bow as if she expected him to applaud and toss coins. She almost giggled again. They'd probably throw her out of the library if she tried a clown dance here, even if it was a "Clowning Around" day.

Carrie rose sedately to her feet, returned the clown books to their shelf, and crossed the concourse into the fiction area.

Again she wandered along, only half-reading titles and author names, content to be enjoying a library— any library. She saw a hallway on her left and turned that way, spotting two rows of computers, every one of them in use. Internet access for library patrons.

A closed, glass-windowed door beside a sign that said *Study Room* caught her eye, and she headed over to investigate, peering through the door's glass into a darkened room with a counter visible on the wall opposite the door.

Study Room? Maybe people signed up to use it for projects. They might even be allowed to lock up at the end of each day's work so books and other research material could be left out until the project was completed.

She tried the door. It wasn't locked, so the space wasn't currently in use. She wondered if it held a comfortable chair, a nice place for reading. All she could see in the dim light from the hall was the counter.

No one was paying any attention to her. Every face in the area stared at a computer screen, so she decided to look inside the room. She opened the door, felt for a light switch, pushed it up.

Carrie wasn't a screaming person, but she couldn't control the gasped air intake that came. The room was indeed occupied. A woman sat in the upholstered chair against the wall that held the door. Blood stained the front of her teal-blue shirt and the chair's upholstery. So much blood. She must be dead, but, just in case—Carrie tiptoed over to the woman, though she couldn't have said why she was trying to be quiet. She put a hand at the pulse point in the woman's throat, waited, felt nothing. The eyes were open, fixed, but the woman's skin was warm.

Then she noticed a badge on the woman's shirt. It identified her as Alisha Vance, Librarian.

Carrie went back to the entrance, turned off the light, shut the door, leaned against the wall.

The library was full of children! She looked at her watch. In about twenty minutes their program would be over. What could she do now without causing a panic? Who was the one to tell?

She had to do *something!*

A key! The study room must be locked quickly. Where was the librarian who had found the clown books for her? Surely he'd know where to get the key.

But she didn't want to leave this door. What if someone else opened it?

She wished her husband was with her. At the last minute he had decided to stay home and catch up on garden work. She suspected he found the twins a bit much, though the dear man would never admit it.

Henry, here with her, could advise about the

proper steps to take next. It was sometimes handy to be married to a retired police officer. He'd know who to contact first and how to talk with them, and she could guard this door while he went for help.

But Henry wasn't here. She was on her own, and she didn't dare use her phone to call the library office. Her conversation could be overheard.

While Carrie thought frantically about what to do next, *Who Cares!* strolled into the hallway and leaned against the wall. Was he waiting for computer time? He eyed Carrie for a moment, then ducked his head and seemed to be staring at a spot on the carpet. Carrie followed his gaze. There really was a spot. Reddish. It could be blood.

Quick. Act. Do something.

"Excuse me, uh, sir."

He looked up and stared at her

I have to say something more.

"Umm, please, do me a favor. I need to stand here for a while. Could you go get a librarian for me?"

He jerked a thumb over his shoulder toward one of the library areas Carrie hadn't yet explored and went back to studying the floor. While she watched, he rubbed his shoe over the spot.

She blew an impatient puff of air she hoped the man heard and walked to the indicated room's wide entrance, turning sideways so she could keep an eye on the door of the study room. A woman was seated at a desk facing her, talking to a boy who looked about fifteen.

Carrie moved two steps into the room and stopped. If she went further, she couldn't stay in control of the study room door. If she got too far away, someone might open the door before she could stop them.

"Excuse me," she said. Then, louder, "Excuse me, could I speak with you over here? I need to keep an eye on something out there." She waved a hand toward the computer area. "I have an important question."

Suddenly Carrie wondered how this woman would react to seeing the body of a fellow librarian so, when she excused herself to the boy and came, Carrie asked only, "Do you have a key to the Study Room? I need to lock the door."

Maybe the woman would think she had signed up to use the room.

"Lock it? The room isn't usually locked."

"Case of priority, the Library Director's instructions." Carrie had no idea what to say the instructions were, and no clue if this nonsense would work.

Thank goodness it did. "Reference Desk," the woman said.

"I am so sorry, I absolutely must stay here. Could you get the key for me?"

The woman gaped at her for a moment. Then, probably deciding a quick trip to get the key would be better than arguing with a peculiar, but possibly director-sanctioned, female, headed toward the reference desk. In a minute she returned with the key.

Carrie sighed in relief, thanked the woman, and locked the door while *Who Cares!* watched her.

Now what? Call 911? No, best to see the library director first. Carrie hoped she was in the building.

Her increasingly frantic appeals at the checkout desk finally convinced the young man on duty that it might be a good idea to interrupt the director, no matter what she might be doing. Almost immediately after his call, a woman came into the concourse and, following the attendant's pointing finger, approached Carrie. She extended her hand, "Francine Morales. How may I help you?"

Carrie looked up and down the concourse and lowered her voice as she shook the director's hand. It was no time to mince words. "I'm Carrie McCrite, and I'm very sorry, but I just found the body of one of your librarians in the study room. Her badge said 'Alisha Vance.' I've locked the door. The police must be called because it looks like the woman was murdered. I guess I don't need to remind you there are children in the building, so maybe as little fuss as possible for now?"

Give the woman something, she was cool. She didn't blink an eye. "Hand me the key, please."

"But..."

Director Morales held out her hand, her face stony. Carrie handed her the key.

Without comment, the woman turned away and headed toward the study room.

"But," Carrie said again, wanting the police to be called right away. Then she realized it was proper for the director to verify what she had been told. She'd never seen Carrie. For all she knew, the director might think she could be dealing with a crackpot—or a murderer.

Carrie hurried after her. Probably Ms. Morales knew enough not to disturb a crime scene, but it might be a good idea to make certain the area stayed as pristine as possible.

When Carrie got to the room, the light was on, the door closed. It wasn't locked, so she walked in, shutting the door behind her and turning the lock's knob. Director Morales faced the dead woman, head down, one hand over her eyes. When she heard Carrie, she looked up.

"She was like this when you found her?"

"Exactly."

"Why did you come in here?" The tone held accusation as well as, Carrie imagined, suspicion.

"This is only the second time I have been in your library. I used to work as a research librarian in the Tulsa City-County Library system, and I'm interested in all libraries. I was looking around while a friend and her grandchildren were at the show featuring Noddy Clown."

The director studied her for a moment. Then she took out a cell phone and speed-dialed a number while Carrie wondered if she'd been changed from body discoverer to murder suspect.

Suspect! Carrie hadn't seen *Who Cares!* when she came through the computer area following Director Morales. What if...the magazine! He'd been reading a slick cover magazine. His fingerprints should be on it, and that might turn out to be important. She'd have to find that magazine, pick it up with a facial tissue wrapped around her fingers, and save it until the police arrived. She looked out the glass door toward where *Who Cares!* had been standing. The spot on the floor was now an almost unnoticeable smudge.

The director's voice interrupted Carrie's thoughts. "The police will be here as soon as possible, and I've asked them to enter through the employee door into the office area. No sirens. As to the children...usually after an event like this, children and their families either leave immediately or stay in their part of the library, browsing through books and games. But, of course, a few may come down here. I'll have someone bring a screen from the office to shield the door glass from the inside, and we'll relock the door. I can't really shut down the computer area and the Teen Scene sections. That would cause too much fuss.

"Now, Ms. McCrite, won't you come with me and wait in my office until the police get here?"

"When will the clown show be over?" Carrie asked.

Morales looked at her watch. "Noddy was late setting up so the show will run about twenty minutes more. Friends of the Library are serving cookies and juice after the finish, and usually almost everyone stays for that. We probably have another thirty to forty minutes."

"I need to find a magazine before I go to your office." In response to a startled look, Carrie explained about *Who Cares!*

"All right. I'll walk with you. Then we can wait in my office."

She wants to keep an eye on me and make sure I stay in the building, Carrie thought, glancing at the woman's troubled face. Maybe she's the teeniest bit afraid of me, too.

* * *

The Library Director's office held a desk, a worktable, and had large windows overlooking the adult library. Director Morales indicated a chair at the table for Carrie, then sat across from her. After she was seated, her eyes strayed into the distance. She said nothing.

She's probably contemplating all she's going to face during the next few hours, Carrie thought, as she put the sports magazine on the table, and asked, "Did you know Alisha Vance well?"

The director came back from her distant thoughts and looked at Carrie in silence for a short time before she said, "No, not really, though I suppose I was closer to her than anyone else in our library. She's only been here with us for about six months, and she was a very private person." There was a pause before the director continued. "You know, I talked with her just a couple of hours ago."

Another pause while Francine Morales studied her fingernails.

"She came to us from Fort Ponder last winter. She'd been director of their library for over twenty years—had the best qualifications. Master of Library Science. Way over-qualified for the position we had open."

"Married? Does she have family here?"

"Never married. That library was her life, her family. She hated leaving there and really wasn't at home here yet. It would be hard, you know, going from directing it all to starting over as a new employee here. She said she had family here and gave that as a reason for coming to us, but she put no names on her application and I have never heard her say anything about a family member."

A clock somewhere behind Carrie ticked several times before the woman across the table spoke again. "Remember when the southern part of the state had all that rain after the hurricane a couple of years ago? The Fort Ponder Library basement flooded, weakening one wall. It collapsed, damaging the building above. They had pumps in the basement removing water, but when the electricity went off, the pumps shut down. I gather no one offered any gasoline-powered ones."

The director stopped speaking again, stared at the tabletop, lined up the edges on a stack of papers, then pushed them aside. She shook her head as if trying to erase a bad dream. Several clock ticks sounded before she continued.

"Alisha had been assured there was adequate insurance for her library, though she'd never seen a policy and couldn't get anyone to show it to her. After the flood, the city recorder tried to find a record of insurance, but nothing turned up.

"Alisha asked permission to search for it herself. I gather she and the city recorder were good friends— she called her Linda—so the woman gave her a key, asked her to keep the search a secret, and stipulated that she report findings only to her. When Alisha was at City Hall one night, trying to make sense of stacks of disorganized documents, she came upon papers showing the library had earned several grants she had applied for. She'd been told they were denied. Searching further, she learned that a city council member had accepted the grant money on behalf of the library. Alisha never saw any of that money.

"Well, Alisha wasn't about to let it go, and the next day she confronted the council member with her information. He acted aghast, fairly convincingly, I gather, and insisted on going over the paperwork himself. She gave him the originals, but made and kept copies, a good thing, since the originals disappeared before the next council meeting and the member insisted he'd never seen them.

"Alisha took her copies to that meeting, plus enough extras for the mayor and each council member. That's when the good old boy network kicked in. The council member resigned quietly, 'to spend more time with his family,' and city officials told Alisha the matter was closed.

"Of course the library received no grant money, and no one ever found any insurance policy. Alisha was blamed for the whole mess, though only through innuendo and gossip since actual malfeasance couldn't be proved. But she was fired anyway.

"To make things worse, she got several hang-up phone calls during the night for the next few weeks. She assumed it was the council member calling and reported the calls to the police, but her appeals for help were ignored.

"After her firing, she applied for library openings around the state. We had an opening, certainly liked her qualifications, and hired her. It was only after she had been here several weeks that she confided in me, telling the story I have just shared with you."

Carrie sat in silence, then said, "That poor woman."

"Yes, it is terribly, terribly sad. And now I'm wondering who to notify about Alisha's murder. Maybe the police can help me find her family.

"But you know what's peculiar, Ms. McCrite? Alisha's friends back in Fort Ponder told her that gossip started about the resigned council member after she left, though it had more to do with an affair with her friend Linda than the library itself. His wife shut him out of their house in March. He owns an auto dealership in Fort Ponder and stayed in town, but Alisha's one-time friend Linda quit her job and disappeared—or moved away—a month later."

"Could that mess have anything to do with Alisha's murder?"

Francine Morales looked startled. "I wouldn't think so. Surely nothing that happened there would be worth killing for. Anyway, it's been over six months now, time for things to quiet down and people to move on."

More silence. Eight more clock ticks. "Still, she's dead. I guess we must deal with why, mustn't we, Ms. McCrite."

"Call me Carrie."

"All right. And I'm Francine." She sighed. "I just

don't know what to think about this. Alisha was such a good, kind person. She was a librarian, for heaven's sake. Who kills librarians?" She laughed, but Carrie didn't smile in response because the laugh expressed no humor.

Instead she said, "I know how hard this is for you. I'm sorry."

"Thank you for understanding." The director fingered her stack of papers again, and her next words came softly, "Some thought Alisha a bit of an odd duck, but she was odd in a way I understood. She loved her library. Being a fanatic about your library is understandable, especially in these days of shrinking budgets and, in some places at least, little support from voters or the government they elect. She felt she was doing important work."

There was a light tap on the door, and before the director could acknowledge it, a wide-eyed young woman stuck her head through the opening. "There are police here. They're asking for you," she said.

* * *

Two uniformed officers waited near the employee entrance. They introduced themselves as Detectives Margie Cardona and Joseph Benton and listened attentively while Director Morales explained the situation, including the presence of at least forty pre-school children in the library. Looking them over, she said, "Having uniformed police officers in the building will stir up more attention than we need."

"Oh, I didn't think of that," Detective Benton said. "Probably officers in plain clothing will be coming later, but for now, we have raincoats in the car, and we do need to see the crime scene as soon as possible."

Detective Cardona had already headed toward the door, and no one said anything until she returned with two trench coats that, Carrie thought, certainly seemed to fit the situation. They looked like coats one might see worn by any detective in a television drama.

Escorted by the director, the officers left for the study room, asking Carrie to wait for them in the library's conference room. She found the room and sat there for several minutes. Then, tired of waiting, she decided to take a quick look at the clown program.

From the concourse she could tell the noise level was relatively low in the children's end of the building and, peeking through the doors, saw Noddy dancing a jerky jig. He held a red and white umbrella over his—oops, her—head. After watching for a moment, she hurried back down the concourse to the conference room. When she opened the solid

wood door, the director and the librarian who'd
found the clown books sat facing her across the
conference table.

Francine introduced the man as Randy Hornbuckle, saying he'd seen Alisha several times during
the morning. "I have asked him to tell us about her
activities. I thought the police might be interested."

"Good idea," Carrie said and settled into a chair,
looking expectantly at Randy.

He glanced at her but spoke to the director. "I
should say that gossip about some tragedy here is
spreading through the library staff, though of course
no one has been told any facts. I think you should
explain what has happened—quietly, of course. But,
do you think anyone else here is in danger? Some
maniac...?"

"The police have already said they think this was
directed only toward Alisha, and they asked us to
wait here for now. I will speak to the staff in small
groups in the break room as soon as I can."

He nodded, then said, "As to this morning, of
course I saw Alisha many times, but when I think
about it now, I guess I didn't see her after about one
o'clock. That didn't alarm me, but probably it should
have. Maybe if I..." He bowed his head for a moment
before going on. "I am very, very sorry I didn't keep

tabs on her."

"That wasn't your job," the director said softly. "Don't even think of blaming yourself for what happened."

He shook his head slowly before continuing. "Everything was routine throughout the morning, both of us answering questions, helping patrons find books, doing some straightening. The average Saturday activities."

Carrie asked, "Did you notice anything unusual at all? Maybe someone she spoke with in a way that wasn't quite normal?"

The director nodded at Carrie but didn't speak.

"Well, nothing I'd call suspicious. Oh, wait. I did see her in a conversation that might be thought of as unusual. There was a man who seemed surly and argumentative. I couldn't hear what he said, but I began walking closer to be sure she had back-up if needed. Before I got there he saw me and turned away toward the magazine racks. She smiled and waved at me as if to say 'thanks' and walked off. We weren't close enough to talk."

Carrie leaned forward in her chair. "What did the man look like? What was he wearing?"

"Ummm, khaki shorts, I think, and a t-shirt with some kind of slogan. He had a dark beard and dark hair. Maybe around fifty or a bit older. Tan skin. His hair could have had some grey, but I wasn't close enough to say for sure. Big pockets in his shorts, and they were pretty full. Bulged. I did see him leaving the library a few minutes before coming in here."

Carrie nodded. He'd described *Who Cares!* "Anything else you noticed? Were there any other people she talked with for longer than the usual time?"

"A friend of hers came to visit an hour or so before the clown program began. They were standing in the concourse laughing together about something, and that caught my attention. I walked toward the sound and saw the two of them smiling and talking. The woman with Alisha glanced at me, put her hand over her mouth like a naughty schoolgirl, then drew Alisha into the Adult Non-fiction racks."

"So Alisha acted like she knew the woman?"

"I thought so, yes, which is one reason I didn't disturb them. The way the woman tugged her into the racks did seem like a familiar gesture, not something a patron you didn't know would do." He hesitated, then said quietly, "I think that's the last time I saw Alisha."

"Could you describe the woman?"

Randy was considering this when the door opened and Detective Cardona came in. "We've called for a supervisor and a crime scene technician," she said. "Detective Benton is still with the body and will remain there until they come."

She pulled out one of the chairs and sat. "I assume all three of you have information to share. Who wants to go first?" She removed a pen and pad of paper from one of her pockets and laid them on the table, as well as a small recorder. "I'll be making a record."

The director took charge. "I can talk about Alisha as a person when you need that, and I spoke with her earlier today, but only concerning library business. All seemed normal then."

She introduced Randy and Carrie, saying, "These two have later information that seems more pertinent to her death. Perhaps Mr. Hornbuckle should tell you what he saw first."

When Randy had repeated his story, the officer asked, "Could you describe the woman?"

He looked at Carrie, and the corners of his mouth turned up a fraction of an inch before he spoke. "I have just been thinking about that. She was fairly young, maybe mid-thirties, but who can tell about women these days? Medium height, no taller than Alisha. Wore light color pants, very tight. They ended above the ankles. I noticed a tattoo on her ankle, I think it was a flower, a rose, maybe. She had on a sleeveless top, white, rather skimpy." He drew a dipping half-circle over the front of his shirt.

"She had blond hair in that tousled style so popular now. I didn't really see her face—she put a hand over much of it when she turned toward me." Again he demonstrated, putting his open hand over the lower part of his face. "I didn't walk into the concourse, but I noticed nothing at all suspicious or peculiar in what I saw. Alisha wasn't acting unusual, just happy. I supposed the woman was someone she knew well, or at least a patron she'd helped many times before. I even thought it might be a relative."

He's good at remembering details about people, Carrie thought, *especially when it's an attractive woman.*

The officer turned a page in the note pad and looked at her. "How about you?"

Carrie described the steps she took after walking into the study room. She told the officer about *Who Cares!,* the spot on the carpet, and the magazine, saying also that she believed *Who Cares!* was the same surly man Roger saw talking to Alisha. Then she asked, "How did she die? I don't mean to be too inquisitive, but the three of us here have a more-than-casual interest, as will all of the library staff. Better to have truth than leave everything open to speculation and gossip."

The Sergeant was silent for a moment, seeming to appraise her, then she said, "Stabbed several times. It looks like she was first hit in the head hard enough to stun her, if not knock her out. A little bit of blood there. We do not think she was conscious of what happened after she was hit, which may be of some comfort to you. The killer probably wanted her to be unconscious so she would not cry out when she saw the knife and was stabbed. From the way her clothing is disturbed, it also looks like she did not sit in the chair on her own but was shoved there."

The door opened, and the young woman who'd announced the arrival of the police earlier ushered in three newcomers, all dressed in street clothing. "The children's program has ended," she said, as she closed the door.

"Will I be needed any more for now?" Carrie asked. "I came here with a friend and her grandchildren, and they'll be ready to go home."

One of the newcomers, a tall, dark man in a suit, said, "If you have information, I'd like to hear it myself and perhaps ask you a few questions, though I'm sure Detective Cardona took good notes. Could you make arrangements to stay? Perhaps you'll tell your friends they can go on home without having to give too much explanation about our situation here? You might say there is a need to deal with something concerning a library patron. One of our officers will drive you home later."

"I am the wife of a retired police major, and I do understand your need," she said. "Yes, of course I'll be happy to stay."

Carrie immediately decided her words were too cheerful and eager sounding for the somber circumstances, but they couldn't be erased now. Never mind. She and Henry had helped solve crimes before. Maybe she could be of help here—without getting in the way of any official investigation, of course. After all, what every one of them wanted was justice for Alisha Vance.

"I'll go and explain the situation to my friend," she said.

* * *

Carrie met Eleanor and the twins coming toward her as soon as she reached the concourse. Her friend looked worried, and the JJ's, hugging her sides, were silent.

"What's wrong?" Carrie asked.

"I was going to ask you the same thing," Eleanor said. "When you weren't at our meeting place and hadn't appeared after we waited for a while, we decided to look for you. The program finished at least fifteen minutes ago."

"I am sorry, something weird came up. Eleanor, I need to stay here at the library for a time. You and the children go on. Someone here will give me a ride home."

"Aunt Carrie?" Jeremy's upturned face was far too serious, and his twin, holding her grandmother's hand, looked just as solemn.

"What is it love? How was the show?"

"Noddy...Noddy...he didn't..."

Eleanor interrupted. "Neither of them liked the program. Beats me why. I had a great time. Children, would you please go sit on that bench where I can see you while I talk with Aunt Carrie for a minute."

After the two had obeyed silently and all too sedately, Eleanor continued. "It started out fine with all the kids, including these two, laughing and singing along. Then, after about fifteen minutes, I noticed Jeremy and Jemima had their heads together and were whispering. For the rest of the program they sat there like bumps on a log and kept looking back at me. After the finish, they refused to go up and shake Noddy's big red hand, and they couldn't wait to leave. I had to talk them into staying for juice and cookies."

"Mmmm, that is peculiar," Carrie said. "Let's go sit on the bench and ask them why. I think Jeremy was about to tell us something on his own anyway."

The two women went to the bench and sat, one on each side of the twins. Carrie looked down at Jeremy's sad face and said, "What's wrong, little love?"

"Noddy wasn't he."

Oh, goodness, she thought, *he noticed Noddy is a woman.*

"Why do you think that?"

"Not right. Noddy knows all his songs right. This, this … didn't. Couldn't do umbrella tricks either. The handle got broken."

"Broken? Oh, my."

"Broken. One stick came out of the other."

"Oh, uh, yes, I see." But Carrie did not see, not yet at least.

Next to her twin, Jemima spoke up. "Musta got his socks dirty and took them off. Supposed to be red socks with clocks. You know, 'Clocks on Socks,' like in the story? I know all about it, I's seen…I saw pictures in our books." She nodded confidently and began looking a little brighter. "This Noddy had a flower picture there. No socks. I sat on the floor, and

I could see. Flower painted on. No socks."

"Yes, I see, I do see," Carrie said as her thoughts settled on the image of a jealous woman who wanted her man all to herself. And, if a scandal over missing funds forced a certain disgraced librarian to leave town, that would remove one obstacle.

"Look there," Jeremy said, pointing toward the Children's Library. "See. No socks."

Carrie leaped to her feet and shouted, "Linda!"

The clown jerked to a halt, turned toward Carrie, then, realizing what she'd just given away, shoved several children aside and began running toward the exit.

Carrie kept shouting. "Somebody, grab that clown, somebody get the police, they're in the conference room. Hurry!" Carrie pushed past library patrons and ran toward the door. *If she could just get there in time!*

Stunned adults stood motionless, gawking, but several children laughed, obviously thinking this was a new game. They hurried forward to cluster around their hero.

The clown dropped her tote bag and used both hands to lift the red and white umbrella by its handle. When her hands were above her head, she hurled the cloth-wrapped metal framework toward the children just as Carrie slammed into her side, spoiling her aim. The umbrella's body went over the children's heads and skittered harmlessly along the floor.

The umbrella handle, with its very thin, very long blade at the end, remained in the clown's hand.

Red and white clown suit arms reached out like a striking snake and wound around Carrie's neck, yanking her against a female body. The dagger pricked at Carrie's throat, a bee sting of pain.

"Back," the clown shrieked. "Everyone get back or I'll cut her throat."

The crowd reversed, rolling back into the concourse as the clown slid nearer the automatic doors, dragging Carrie with her. The few remaining adults grabbed for loose children who were still laughing and pointing at the clown. Two or three toddlers began wailing their displeasure at having to leave this game.

Carrie, intent on keeping the clown away from the children, hadn't reacted quickly enough in her own defense. She now allowed the woman to drag her along, but made herself a dead weight, hoping to delay things until the police arrived. Carrie was no sylph, but Linda was strong. She wasn't even breathing heavily, though her movements slowed.

If only I had taken time to get the police first, Carrie

thought, *if only I'd had more time to think.*

After all, she now knew who was inside the clown suit, and she knew who had killed Alisha Vance. Maybe she should have let her get away. The police could always find her later.

Where were the police?

* * *

The clown pulled Carrie through the entrance alcove and out the doors onto the sidewalk. Then they were crossing the parking lot. Carrie's shoe heels made a harsh, scraping noise on the paving, matching the now gasping breaths from Linda, who had begun muttering. After a few words, Carrie realized Linda was talking to her.

"How did you know? Did Alisha tell you? No, she couldn't have, she didn't talk to anyone after we had our little reunion." The woman paused, grunted, tightened her arm around Carrie, started moving again. "She was so glad to see me. She meant it, she hugged me. After that, I was sorry I had to go ahead and kill her. But there was Donald to think about. He wouldn't come with me, wouldn't divorce that wife of his, and it turned out Alisha was in my way, too.

"Donald said, in spite of everything that happened, he admired Alisha Vance, how well she ran the library on a small budget, how smart she was to do that. He raved about her devotion to the library and the kids that used it. He said his son loved going to the library, said Alisha helped the little brat with his homework. Donald said his son loved Alisha.

"*Loved her!* I thought then that he might love her, too, since he goes sloppy over anything his kid even talks about."

The sight of a clown dragging a woman sent a teenager with a stack of books hurrying back into his car. Carrie hoped he had a smart phone and would use it quickly to call police. *No, that wasn't right. The police were already here, for heaven's sake.*

Linda kept dragging. Carrie's left shoe fell off.

Then the two of them were across the parking lot, stopped next to a blue van. Linda used her body to shove Carrie against the side of the van while she reached back and opened the driver's door with her left hand, still holding the dagger against Carrie's neck with her right. Carrie could see through the gap by the driver's seat and what she saw horrified her. Two feet in red socks with clocks stuck out of a rope-tied blanket roll in the back of the van.

Noddy! Was he dead?

Logic took over. There would have been no need to tie him up if he was dead.

Then she saw one of the feet wiggle. *Thank God.*

Linda continued to lean against Carrie while holding the dagger firmly against her neck, but she didn't make any attempt to get in the van. Her body began twitching nervously, making Carrie's position more perilous.

She obviously didn't plan to take a hostage here, and is probably wondering whether to kill me or let me go.

Carrie began a silent prayer, then looked toward the library doors as a cluster of people came out, walking along the sidewalk on the other side of the parking lot. The group crossed the lot cautiously, still in a cluster. It looked like they were heading for cars near the van. They were eager to get away, and Carrie didn't blame them.

The crowd kept moving. She heard an engine start.

Without warning Linda jerked into action, knocking Carrie to the pavement and kicking at her, pushing her away. Carrie rolled into fetal position as soon as she was on the ground, so the clown's blows struck her back. She heard the van door hinges squeak and raised her head. Was Linda actually leaving? *Yes, she'd lifted a foot to get in the van. Where were the police?*

Then Carrie heard Eleanor yelling, "*Jemima you*

come back here right this minute," as a small sandal appeared from the other side of the still open door and kicked hard at Linda's bare ankle. Linda yelped and began falling. The van door slammed inward, pinning her between the edge of the seat and the metal doorframe.

At last Sergeant Benton was there, bending down as Carrie struggled to her knees. Behind them voices shouted, there was a scuffle, and Sergeant Cardona's voice said, "Gotcha."

Benton helped Carrie stand, then guided her out of the narrow aisle between vehicles and onto the curb.

It took a moment for dizziness to pass and for her feet and legs to be ready to hold her.

"Carrie!"

She looked up. Eleanor, Jeremy, and Jemima stood under a tree in front of the van, cheeks flushed, clothing more than a little mussed. Jemima's overall strap was torn loose.

"I kicked the bad clown in the foot," Jemima said. "I yanked away from Nana and kicked hard before Nana slammed the door on him. He didn't even see me. All those people came out of the library with us, but I was the one who kicked."

Jeremy lifted his chin. "I woulda kicked if I got there first."

Eleanor asked, "Are you okay?"

"Recovering quickly, thank you. I think there are a few dagger pricks on my neck, though. Are they bleeding on my shirt?"

When Eleanor shook her head, Carrie went on. "So you're the one who slammed the door on Noddy?"

"Yep," Eleanor said, "I sure did, though at first I was just chasing after Jemima."

"Nana?" Jeremy looked up at his grandmother.

"Yes, dear."

"Wanna be Pooh Bear for Hollereen."

"Pooh, too," said Jemima.

BUT THEY'RE NOT <u>REALLY</u> DEAD

The constant "pock-pocka-pock" of the muskets wasn't so bad. The boom of the cannons—from this distance at least—was endurable, especially for someone who had listened to rock drummers turned up loud. But the wind was sending black powder smoke straight toward them and, in this heat, that was awful. The whole idea was stupid and awful. She was hot, sweaty, and she'd had enough.

Out on the field, men were playing at dying. You could hear their screams and moans above the other noises of battle. They were certainly realistic about it. Just a few minutes ago, as a charge was surging forward in front of them, there had been a sharp crack—an odd sound for a musket, she thought. Before that there was an almost female-sounding cry, the name "David." Surely a name wasn't what she really heard.

After the shot, a man right in front of them dropped to his knees and collapsed on the ground, too hard, too realistically. Ouch! These men got way too wrapped up in play-acting at war. Idiot. He might have cracked his head open.

The man was still there, of course. No medics were around during the heat of this battle. She stared at the fallen soldier, not twenty yards away, with the grey cap tilted sideways over his eyes. He was in full sun, probably risking heat stroke. Playing at war wearing wool uniforms in Arkansas in July was beyond stupid. It might be authentic, but it was stupid.

Quite a few of the casualties were choosing to fall in the shade of the pasture's trees. That showed some degree of sense, at least. Maybe this man's captain, or general, or whatever the man running this re-enactment was called, had suggested where and when he should die. She wondered what would happen if, without instructions, every single soldier here decided to be shot at the same time and the whole army toppled over. Would some of them have to get up, say, "Oops, my mistake," and begin their forward charge again? Perhaps they had been given slips of paper saying who was to be wounded, and when and where that should happen. But that would assume they all wore watches and could look at them.

Carrie straightened the straw hat balanced on her grey curls, shifted position in her green canvas folding chair, and glanced over at the two people sitting next to her. They wouldn't care if she left. She could walk over to the Sutler's Camp area. She didn't need any 1860's style merchandise, but sutlers and their battlefield supply camps were a part of Civil War history too, and they had to be a lot more interesting than soldiers playing at dying in heat and smoke.

Henry, her husband, would understand if she left. In fact, he might be wishing he could leave too. He'd told her only yesterday that his military service and long career in the Kansas City Police Department had cured him of any interest in gun battles, including those copying the Civil War. Even when she and Henry got involved in their "Ma and Pa Kettle detective work," which was what her son Rob called their avocation, Henry rarely carried a gun. He said they'd leave firearms to the licensed law.

The only reason Henry had come here today was because his daughter Susan was here. Susan was here because her husband was out on the field, helping re-enact the 1862 Battle at Pea Ridge, Arkansas. Ah-ha. Carrie decided she could ask him about who died and when after all this was over.

She fanned vigorously with her program and looked back at the Confederate soldier lying in the grass in front of them. Well, he might have to bake in the sun, but Carrie McCrite did not.

She reached over to put her hand on Henry's arm. "I'd like to get away from this for a while and walk over to the Sutler's Camp. Want to come along?"

He looked down, laid his hand over hers, and squeezed lightly as he smiled. "Go shopping? No thanks. I'll stay here with Susan. You won't get lost? There must be several thousand people here."

"The program says this battle will last at least another hour, so I can be back before the end." After pursing her lips to send him a silent kiss, which he returned, she popped out of her chair and headed toward the camp area.

As she walked through the coarse pasture grass that smelled of heat and dust and—faintly—of cow, Carrie pictured the rows of soldiers marching across here early this morning. It was amazing how many bellies had bulged against uniform buttons, and there were quite a few heads with grey hair. All men, of course. Surely no woman would choose to hide her identity in a wool uniform and play soldier in this heat.

Still, if they wanted to, it should be allowed.

She knew that some women, masquerading as men, had fought beside brothers and husbands on real Civil War battlefields. But now?

She had to admit it might be fun to see if she could pass as a soldier—in cooler weather, of course. But she'd probably have to cut her hair. The springing white curls would ruin it for her, as well as...she looked down at the two bumps pushing out the front of her Arkansas Razorback t-shirt. Well, maybe wearing heavy wool would flatten her front enough to pass.

Ah, well, on to the Sutler's Camp. Playing war was for younger women. They should be allowed into re-enactment groups as soldiers if they wanted to be there, but even today it wasn't always allowed. Susan said her husband's group wouldn't admit women as soldiers. Phooey on them.

She trudged on behind rows of spectators' chairs and eventually came to a line of white supply tents that stretched for more than a block on each side of the makeshift grassy main street. Women in traditional 1860's dress were everywhere, and children in overalls and straw hats, or miniature full skirts and bonnets, played with hoops and balls and rag dolls, filling the street with color, motion, and happy shouts. A few spectators, evidently bored with the battle like she had been, were roaming about. This was certainly going to be better than the noise and smoke and play-like death going on behind her.

Wandering from tent to tent, Carrie looked at canned goods with 1860's labels, iron cooking pots, blankets, guns, and trappings for horses. She lingered in one tent that displayed women's period clothing, fabric, dress patterns, and some amazingly nice antique-looking buttons and jewelry. Leaving there, she came to a small tent with a closed flap. Odd. She wondered what was inside and was tempted to open the flap and look inside. She stood there, staring at the closed tent flap, and thinking about the displays of goods for sale she had seen.

Of course there had been no peddlers at the real Pea Ridge battle in March of 1862. The men fighting there had marched for days through sleet and snow. Their supply of food was almost gone. Most of the Confederates were teenaged southern farm boys, poorly dressed for winter in the Ozarks, since wool uniforms were not available for all back then. Some of the soldiers wore shoes with holes, others had no shoes at all, just rags tied around their feet. When they could, Civil War soldiers stole shoes, coats, and food from the dying and dead—whether enemy or comrade.

For a moment, Carrie shut her eyes and thought of those long-ago boys. An icy day. Little or no sleep.

If they rested, there was only frozen ground with patches of snow. Nothing to eat. Their commander, Major General Van Dorn, had marched them too far ahead of their supply wagons in his hurry to get behind the Union lines for an attack.

Someone touched her arm. "You feeling faint, lady? Too much sun? Come in the tent and sit."

Carrie turned to see sad blue eyes behind round, brass-rimmed spectacles. Beard. Overalls with a strap twisted over one shoulder. He'd dressed in a hurry. A sutler. He pointed toward the small tent with the now-open flap. "Come on in and rest."

"Goodness, thank you, I will. But I'm alright. I was just thinking...back."

He nodded as he led the way into the tent. "Oh, yes, I see. Gets to you. You can understand why sometimes re-enactors are so carried away they hurt each other. Medics occasionally treat real wounds from bayonets, swords, knives. Thank God they don't have actual bullets out on the field. All those guns..."

He pointed at two folding chairs but said no more after they were seated. Facing him, Carrie thought his eyes seemed to be watching something miles away.

Then the dreamy look vanished, and he waved his arm in the direction of the battle noise. "Did you know there was a woman here then? Mary Whitney Phelps. The only woman known to be at the Pea Ridge battle other than a teenage girl hiding in the basement of Elk Horn Tavern. Used the tavern as a hospital. It's said blood dripped through the floorboards on that poor girl."

For a moment the sad eyes turned icy, reflecting the horror Carrie felt, but it passed, and he went on.

"Mary Phelps came south from Springfield with a wagon load of supplies for her husband's company. He was Colonel John Phelps, leading the 25th Missouri for the Union. Later he'd be Missouri Governor Phelps.

"How Miz Phelps made it here with supplies through all those bands of loose soldiers and guerilla warriors only she could tell us. But she did it, then got cut off when Van Dorn's Confederates attacked from the north. She stayed right in the thick of things. She could shoot, and it's said she did. The story told is that she fought, nursed, passed out food and supplies from her wagon, even tended her own husband after he was wounded."

Carrie repeated the name slowly, "Mary Whitney Phelps. I've never heard of her, but I guess I shouldn't be surprised that a woman like her wasn't recognized." She stopped, testing his reaction, but he was staring into space again so, to bring him back, she asked a question. "What did Mary Phelps wear here?"

The question surprised him and brought his eyes back to her face. "Oh, well, I don't know. No pictures of her have been found, if any ever existed. I'd guess a mid-length, plain skirt over men's trousers. That's what nurses often wore. No hoops or extra petticoats. A jacket, much like the men wore, and a shirtwaist. Probably men's boots. Don't forget she was driving a team pulling a loaded wagon."

"A true *she-ro,*" she said. "Thanks for telling me about her."

She hesitated a moment before going on. "So there weren't, as far as anyone knows, women who fought here other than Mary Phelps?"

The man's expressive eyes showed he didn't like her question. "Well, I really wouldn't know about that."

Carrie pressed ahead. "What about today? Could there be any women masquerading as men out on the battlefield today?"

In the silence, the eyes behind the round lenses spoke of fear. Why? After all, he had brought up Mary Phelps, a woman in battle. Carrie wasn't asking him to reveal secrets that would hurt anyone.

But he said nothing, and, sensitive to his mood, Carrie changed the subject. Waving her hand around the shelves of magazines, books, and paper goods in the tent, she asked, "You do this as a business?"

"Only on re-enactment weekends and during the summer. I'm a high school history teacher in St. Louis. My wife kept up our stock before she was killed last March. Auto accident."

"Oh, I am so sorry."

"Yes." The blue eyes disappeared behind closed lids. "A wreck. She was in a car with a man who was driving drunk. It spun, went in a ditch, and she was killed."

There was a pause, and while Carrie wondered what to say next, the man spoke again, whispering, "He had only a few bruises."

After murmuring, "Terrible, terrible thing," Carrie waited through a long silence until, not wanting to simply walk away from this sad man, she returned to a subject that seemed to interest him most.

"I have heard that Pea Ridge was a decisive battle win for the Union."

"Oh, yes. It was about who would control St. Louis and the Mississippi River. If the Confederates had won here, and they almost did, this part of the country might be the Confederate States of America now. At the time, there was not much between here and St. Louis to stop them. The Confederates had won the battle at Wilson's Creek in Missouri in August 1861."

Two women in wide, swinging skirts came into the tent and asked to see letter paper. The sutler nodded to Carrie and turned away to help his customers. The conversation was over.

She stayed in the tent for a few minutes, watching the man as he pulled out boxes. He seemed to be such a gentle, sensitive person. What beautiful, wavy hair he had. Carrie loved touching Henry's wavy, grey-streaked black hair, and, because of that, she often noticed other men's hair. The sutler's hair was white-blond. His above-the-ears hair was mashed flat in a band that circled the back of his head. Hat hair, Henry called it. Too bad. The brim imprint on the sutler's head spoiled the flow of pale, silky waves.

After a last glance at him, Carrie moved on.

There was a revival-sized tent across from the small canvas shelter where the history teacher sold his 1860's paper goods. The big tent's flap was wide open, and wooden forms displaying various military uniforms stood on either side of the opening. The forms were fully dressed, even to white gloves. Carrie, now curious about uniforms, went in.

There didn't seem to be anyone minding the tent, and, after a quick scan of the area, she began to browse, lifting stacked uniforms to look at buttons and trim, inspecting the construction of jackets and pants. A few pairs of pants had modern zippers. Carrie knew purists would reject these, but why did it matter? Surely no man would be unfastening his pants in public. She would go for convenience every time.

Carrie was looking at fancy braid on an officer's jacket when she heard someone come into the tent. She was behind a clothing rack, so she pushed jackets aside to peer through.

Well, now. It was the sad-eyed history teacher, and he was laying a folded Confederate uniform jacket and hat on the counter. That was all the man did. By the time Carrie had taken a breath and opened her mouth to speak, the paper goods sutler was gone. As he left, Carrie heard a male voice just outside the tent say, "Hey there, Simon. Good crowd, hm? Selling a lot? Hey, I was sorry to hear David only got probation. Doesn't seem right, does it!"

Her spine began a familiar tingling. David? A soldier's uniform?

Well, none of her business. Henry said curiosity about things that did not concern her could lead to trouble she might not be equipped to handle. But then, it could also lead to interesting treasure hunts.

She sighed. This wasn't the time or place to suppose some kind of mystery that did not concern her.

But, who was David?

Shaking her shoulders to quiet her spine, Carrie left the tent.

She continued along the grassy street, then, glancing at her watch, decided she had time to see the army encampment spread over rolling hills beyond the sales tents. Rows of small tents covered this area. There were campfires for cooking, but at least the wood smoke was fragrant. Women and a few soldiers were scattered about, sitting quietly on blankets or stools, talking, caring for equipment and guns, or, in the case of the women, often doing needlework. Since it was nearing noon, several were bending over campfires. Flags marking the camp locations of various fighting units fluttered in the breeze.

Children responded to her greeting but, for the most part, men and women ignored her, keeping at their work or conversation as if they were actors in a play—which, on a massive scale, they really were. It was easy to get lost in history here—easier, really, than it had been next to the battlefield. Here, history surrounded her, women's history that she understood. Here, movement was slow, relaxed, and relaxing, quite unlike movement on the battlefield.

Voices, many of them revealing southern accents, were slow and relaxed too. Carrie paid no attention to the words, but was content to move among the soothing murmur. Then she was out of the busy area and walking past tents that were obviously empty. So, only various groups of male re-enactors stayed here, and all of them were in this morning's battle.

A fair-haired soldier came through the trees bordering the battlefield and hurried down the row of tents. He looked pre-occupied and seemed not to see her or hear her spoken greeting. Well, of course. Soldiers playing a part here wouldn't speak to a woman wearing an Arkansas Razorback t-shirt. But his hurry was such a contrast to everything else in this encampment that she turned her head to watch him. Just before ducking to enter his tent, he took off his grey cap to expose long hair falling in white-blond waves.

Carrie continued to the end of the tent area, turned around, and began walking back. There was motion inside the soldier's tent, a swishing of fabric. The tent flap parted, and a face looked out, ducked back in. It was a woman wearing a blue, sprigged-print gown.

Carrie had arrived back among the cooking fires, playing children, and women with their needlework when a woman in a sprigged-print gown and matching blue sunbonnet swished past her, headed toward the sutler's area. Her hands held her skirts up on both sides so she could move more quickly. Carrie wanted to bet she was heading toward the paper-goods tent.

She'd have won the bet.

Pausing outside the tent, Carrie decided she needed some unique letter paper for a Christmas gift. Stepping as quietly as she could, she walked through the open flap.

The woman was facing away from the tent flap, the man was in profile, his head slanted toward the back wall of the tent.

"It's over. I'm glad I was there. I was pretty sure you could not pull the trigger against him. But we both wanted assurance that the drunken devil was never going to kill another person."

The woman's voice softened. "It's better this way Simon. You are such a good man, too good for messing with this sort of thing. Being with him may have been Carol's choice, but he was still a murderer. Don't forget that. Don't grieve for him."

The man's face was so pale it almost faded into the white tent behind him. He put his hands up in protest, then moved them over his face.

She was almost whispering now, "David is gone. It's ended."

Carrie slowly backed up the few steps toward the tent opening, then turned and hurried toward Henry, the green folding chairs, and the soldier lying on the ground in front of them.

Had real medics looked at that man yet?

And Henry was so right. There were some things better left to the licensed law. Some things Carrie McCrite just wasn't equipped to handle. Henry was going to have to help her understand what to do next.

TRACKER

Thump!

Carrie put the last grocery bag on the kitchen table and went to hang up her jacket. Grocery shopping was not her favorite chore—that is, unless Henry was with her. He made a game of it, like mispronouncing names printed on cans and inventing bizarre recipes and other uses for perfectly normal items like frozen peas. She chuckled, thinking of what he sometimes said about those. Softballs for mice using shoestring potatoes as bats was okay, but a few other ideas? Oh, no! The chuckling softened into a smile.

Carrie was still smiling when she returned to the kitchen and put fresh vegetables in the sink. When the other groceries were tended to, she began peeling and chopping the potatoes, onions, carrots, and celery that were going in the pot of broth just beginning to simmer on the stove.

When she opened the front door to take her bowl of peelings to the compost pile, she stopped short.

What was a bright red candy bar wrapper doing on the porch floor?

Oh! Probably Henry found the wrapper when he was mowing somewhere around the area. It could have blown in from the road. He probably came to get a drink from the thermos he'd left on the porch and dropped it here to add to the trash later. Oh, well. She hurried on toward the compost container and then saw that the outdoor water faucet on the house wall was dripping. What? Henry again? Washing hands or boots? Some ordinary explanation, of course. She turned off the water drip and picked up the wrapper before going back inside the house.

Carrie was popping a pan of pop-tube biscuits in the oven when Henry, fresh from a shower, came in, sniffed, said, "Umm," and kissed the top of her head before saying anything more.

"All is well around the place. I am not looking forward to leaf removal, which is coming soon, but we're all mowed, probably for the last time this year. I added a bag of leaves that had already fallen to the compost and saw your peelings, so I figured out what supper was going to be. How about I set the table?"

"Good, but leave the large bowls here. We can fill them from the pot on the stove. By the way, did you find a candy bar wrapper while you were mowing and leave it on the porch?"

"Candy bar wrap—no. Why?"

"There was one there when I got home from the grocery. And the outside water faucet was dripping."

"Huh. Odd. Did we have a visitor? I was out of sight of the house most of the time, so it could have happened. Someone lost and looking for instructions to an address, maybe? I don't think the Jehovah's Witness visitors would leave a candy wrapper if they were here. They'd have left a leaflet."

"True." She turned back toward the sink. "Oh my gosh! There's a big dog crossing our driveway, nose to the ground, and two people walking down the lane."

Henry came to the window. "I wonder. Could that be a tracking dog? If so, it might explain the candy wrapper and dripping faucet. We did have a visitor, and those folks are looking for him. Or her. Whatever. I saw no one while I was mowing, but then, the visitor would have heard the mower and stayed away from wherever I was at the time—if they were trying to avoid discovery, that is. But then, why the wrapper?"

He was interrupted by a series of loud barks.

"Whoo, guess that was some kind of knock,"

Carrie said, as she followed Henry toward the front door.

A man and woman in dark outdoor clothing and boots stood on the porch. The man held a leash, now fastened on the dog's harness.

"Hello, I'm Josh Parker, and this is Margo Khatri." He put a hand on the dog's head. "And this is Tracker. Not a very original name, because he is a tracking dog. Margo and I are members of a K-9 search and rescue team. We're searching for a Caucasian woman and man in their 40s. Have you seen them, by chance? Tracker tells us at least one of them came here and stood on this porch."

Henry nodded, introduced himself and Carrie, and said, "I think they may have been here, but neither of us saw them." He opened the door wider. "Won't you come in?"

"Thanks, but we'll only be a minute more. No need to take Tracker in your house."

Carrie said, "When I came home from the grocery store a couple of hours ago, I found a candy bar wrapper on the porch floor in front of where Tracker is sitting now. And our outdoor faucet was dripping. Water in that area showed it had been used recently."

Margo Khatri said, "If you have the wrapper, could you get it? Tracker verified the scent of our couple at your water faucet before coming up on the porch. He can identify the wrapper as well."

When Carrie returned with the candy wrapper, she gave it to Margo and, after Tracker had sniffed and given a short bark, Josh Parker said, "Yup, your visitors were our couple."

Henry said, "I was mowing on the other side of the hollow. I didn't hear or see anyone. Is there something we can do to help? Who are these people?"

"Married couple. He was on the County Sheriff's trustee work gang picking up trash along County Road 18 near here. His wife drove up, swerved toward the workers, and screamed out the open windows as if she'd lost control of the car. Everyone, including the guarding deputy, scattered. Everyone but her husband, that is. He jumped in, and they roared off. Deputies found the empty car, which turned out to be rented, near Spring Creek Road a short time later. Since Tracker, Margo, and I had just finished finding a lost child in the forest over near Dawson, we said we'd stay out a few more hours and help search for the couple."

Henry said, "The fellow's crime must have been fairly light if he was okayed for a work crew."

"It was light, even ridiculously so. The guy was charged with making a threat with a dangerous weapon, his first offense, but the person he threatened was a belligerent sort, a city council member in Bonny, and he wasn't about to let the guy get away with challenging him."

"What was the weapon?"

Josh Parker laughed. "A hard-cover notebook. They were at a council meeting. He'd come to protest placing a dirt mine near his home. Turns out the mine is scheduled for land the council member owns."

"And, of course," Henry said, "the council member is set to make some money from that transaction, so he took exception. But a notebook? I can't believe they arrested him for that."

"Well, he did hit the guy on the arm with the hard edge of the thing, and it did cause a bruise. He said that the hit was an accident caused when the council member grabbed him on that arm, but who knows?"

"Oh, of all the...well, we'll stay alert. Do you have a number we can call if we have any information?"

"Tracker will probably find them before long, but just in case." He handed Henry a card with his number on it. "Thanks for your help. Guess we'll set off again. Thanks."

* * *

Carrie and Henry were finishing supper cleanup

when Josh, Margo, and Tracker re-appeared. "Lost them," Margo said. "That road up the hill behind here? They must have met a car there because Tracker lost the scent. We asked the folks at the houses along the road, and no one was missing a vehicle, though one of them had a truck with the keys in it parked beside the house. Our couple is probably many miles away by now, and we've done all we can, so we're heading home, but thought we should update you first. If you do see or hear of them, call the County Sheriff's office."

"Okay," Henry said. "How about I give you a ride to wherever you're parked."

"That would be great. I admit we've had about enough hiking for one day."

* * *

After breakfast the following morning, Carrie said, "It's so pretty out, think I'll hike across the creek and up to Bobcat road. I'd like to check on Sonita and the baby. I think her mother-in-law went home last weekend. Want to come along?"

"No, thanks. I need to finish getting our winter garden planted. I am determined to teach you to like fresh kale. But I also have three kinds of lettuce to go under the portable plastic garden cover. I want to test what winters best. And there's still plenty of

Swiss chard. How about I fix some of that for supper? I'll put a couple of sweet potatoes in to bake and we can finish the left-over baked ham."

"Good. Peanut butter and crackers and peach gelatin for lunch okay? Wouldn't want to spoil our appetites for supper."

"I think I'll make a tuna salad sandwich. I could make enough for two."

She laughed. "Not in the mood for peanut butter? Okay, tuna it is. See you in an hour or so."

Carrie grabbed her walking stick and headed downhill toward the creek. It was small enough that she could hop over or use a well-placed rock if she needed to step in the middle.

Fall and winter were her favorite times for woodland hikes. There was little bother from ticks or chiggers, and she loved seeing bare tree branches outlined against the sky. She thought of them as tree lace.

It was too early for bare branches, but still a pleasant hike, and she looked for remaining wildflowers as she climbed the hill on the other side of the creek, hoping to see the tiny white blossoms of lady's tresses spiraling on their stems. She often found them on this hill in early fall, as well as the blackish pokeweed berries—if the deer hadn't eaten all of them.

Ah-ha, pokeberries over there. She finished the climb singing "Poke Salad Annie" to herself, though what "gators got your granny" had to do with gathering and eating poke weed she did not know. Oh, well. Granny rhymed with Annie.

When she got to the road at the top of the hill, she noticed scattered gravel and a disturbed place on the road's cul-de-sac, almost like someone had been in a hurry and spun their tires. But who hurried on this road? She pushed some of the gravel back in place with her foot, then returned to her song and was singing one of the many verses when she arrived at Sonita and Will's front door and heard baby Summer wailing. So, maybe she could sing "Poke Salad Annie" to six-week-old Summer. A baby would not be picky about her voice or choice of words.

She stopped singing when Sonita opened the door, holding a red-faced Summer cradled in her left arm. "Oh, Carrie, it's great to see you, but..."

"Here, let me take Summer, I have a song to sing to her."

"Well, come on in then. You'll have to sing loud. She's been trying to wear out all our ears. My mom and dad are here for a visit, and look how she's carrying on. She's nursed, we've all held, rocked, and, come to think of it, have done about everything <u>but</u> sing. Summer Pierce, please hush." Sonita jiggled the baby on her arm a couple of times, then, after Carrie had dropped her walking stick in the umbrella stand, handed over the squalling infant. That's when Carrie noticed the couple sitting on the couch. Oops, and she had promised to sing.

Oh, well. She went to sit in the chair with a quilt over it, nodded, and smiled at the couple, who hardly looked old enough to be Sonita's parents and, well, nothing ventured, began singing, hoping the grand-parents would not take offense at the words.

When she got to the chorus, she was astounded when the couple on the couch joined in:
"Poke Salad Annie,
Gators got your granny.
Everybody thought it was a shame
That your mama was working on a chain gang."
After they had repeated the chorus together, all of them began laughing as Carrie looked down at the quiet baby she was holding.

"Sonny," the woman said, "do you still have your Elvis recording of that song? I think Summer likes it. Imagine that, she's responded to good-old-fash-ioned southern rock and roll."

"Don't know about rock and roll," Sonita said,

reaching for her daughter, "but I'll start the CD real low and try putting her in her crib."

Carrie and Sonita's parents waited in silence while Carrie looked around the room, enjoying its somewhat worn, but homey feel. The first time she'd visited Sonita and Will she'd been glad to see that the young Pierces were enjoying comfortable family hand-me-downs.

After Sonita came back in the room the silence from down the hall continued, and she said, "Well, who would have thought? Elvis!

"Oh, excuse my manners. Mom, Dad, this is my through-the-woods neighbor, Carrie McCrite. She and her husband live that way on the other side of the hollow." She pointed in the general direction. "Carrie, meet Marie and Levi Arnson."

"We are very pleased to meet you," Marie Arnson said. "So, you live in the woods over there." She looked at her husband before she continued. "I'm glad Sonita has friends in the area, especially now that she's home during the day. I guess you know she had a good job at Tyson but decided to be a stay-at-home mom after Summer came. Of course, William is home in the evenings and on weekends, but days can seem long when you're by yourself with a newborn."

Carrie said, "So, do you live at some distance? I never heard Sonita say where she's from."

"Oh, we're not too far, but it's been hard for Levi to get away from his job for more than a Sunday, so we can't visit as often as we'd like. He's on a bit of a vacation now, so we headed here to visit Summer, Sonita, and Will. Levi hadn't seen or held Summer yet. Time for him to connect with his first grandchild."

"Well, yes," Carrie said. "How long can you stay?"

"Probably through next week," Marie said. "Levi is good at carpentry, and he can do a bit of work for Sonita while we're here, adding toy shelves in Summer's room, that sort of thing. I plan to give the house a good, deep cleaning that Sonita hasn't had time or energy for. I'll also take over much of the cooking, and, this afternoon, Levi and I get to stay with Summer while Sonita goes out to do grocery shopping. It's our first time babysitting for our grandchild."

Carrie nodded. "That's good for all of you."

Sonita sat on the couch between her parents, putting an arm around each of them. "It sure is. That is, unless Will falls in love with Mom's cooking and realizes my deficiencies."

Her mother gave an old-fashioned snort. "Honey,

you're a good cook, and besides, he's so much in love with you he wouldn't know if you served him TV dinners every night, as long as you were sitting at the table with him."

Sonita's father spoke up for the first time. "As an observing male, I agree with that, but still, Sonny, no reason not to follow the recipes in the notebook your mother brought. They're some of her best."

"Speaking of food, time for me to be heading home. Henry is making tuna salad for lunch. Unlike you, Marie, I am not an accomplished cook. I even brought oatmeal cookies from the store as my 'welcome to the neighborhood' offering for Sonita and Will."

"And, delicious they were," Sonita said. "Carrie, I hope you can come back for another visit while Mom and Dad are still here. And bring Henry."

"I'll plan on it, but I'll give you a call first to be sure it's a good time. Oh, I don't see a car. Did you folks fly here?"

"Oh no," Sonita said, "they drove. I had them drive in the garage when they came. Their car is almost new, so I gave it the place of honor."

"Makes sense," Carrie said. She retrieved her walking stick and left.

* * *

"Not like you to do so much serious thinking," Henry said as they were eating lunch. "So, problems with Sonita and the baby?"

"Oh, no. Everything is fine, except Summer was crying when I got there and, I gather, had been doing so for some time. Sonita's parents are visiting, and it sounded like they'd been trying to quiet her with about everything they could think of, except singing to her."

She told him about seeing pokeberries, which had started her singing, and that, eventually, had quieted the baby.

"Indeed."

"Yes, and Sonita's parents know the song, because when I got to the chorus, they joined in."

"Interesting. Kid's got good taste. So, where do Sonita's parents live?"

"I asked, but they never said. Not across country, I'd guess. They drove here. Just arrived yesterday. They both plan to help with chores around the house while they're here."

"Indeed. So, I assume they are not grey-haired folks with canes."

She laughed. "Oh, no, very young-looking, as grandparents usually are these days. But you can see for yourself, since Sonita said she hoped the two of us would come for a visit while they're still here. Now, tell me, how did the gardening go? Seeds all planted?"

* * *

On Friday, Henry called a friend in the County Sheriff's office and asked if they had found the couple from the work crew abduction. "They assume the couple is far away and, with other problems they're working on, finding them is far from a high priority," he told Carrie. "In fact, realizing he was being laughed at for making such a silly charge about the notebook attack, the council member withdrew his charges. The department is, however, still mildly concerned about the escape from the work crew."

As they were driving to church on Sunday, Henry suggested they plan a walk to visit Sonita and her parents the following day, since the weather forecast predicted sun and moderate temperatures. A phone call to Sonita on Monday morning told Carrie a visit would be welcome, but, after a short hesitation, Sonita said it would save her a trip into town if they wouldn't mind driving Henry's truck rather than walking. That way, they could visit the lumber yard and pick up pre-cut boards and a can of paint ordered by her father for the shelving in Summer's room. She said the items were already charged to the Pierce's account and promised a lunch prepared by her mother as a thank you.

When Henry drove up in front of the Pierce's home, the garage door opened. Sonita came out to show where the lumber should go on the garage floor, next to her parents' car.

"Is her father handicapped?" Henry asked after Sonita had finished helping with the unloading and had gone back in the house without inviting them to come in through the garage.

"Not that I could tell," Carrie said as they pulled up in the parking area next to Sonita's car and went to the front door.

Both grandparents were standing and greeted them warmly after Sonita introduced Henry. Marie excused herself to join Sonita in the kitchen, leaving the two men and Carrie alone in the living room.

"So," Henry said, "you must be good at carpentry. That's a great skill to have. I admit I have only minimal acquaintance with hammers and saws, though I can manage to hang pictures and tighten loose drawer handles."

After chuckles, Levi Arnson said, "Oh, I am guessing you can accomplish more than that. Sonita says you're retired, so you could possibly find time to explore carpentry. What was your profession, if you don't mind me asking?"

Before Henry could answer, Carrie spoke up. "He retired as a major in the Kansas City Police Department. He still has connections with the County Sheriff's Department here."

After what seemed to Carrie an awkward pause, Levi said, "How interesting. Law Enforcement is quite a demanding career, I imagine."

"It can be," Henry said. "And you?"

"I work in a business that, among other things, builds furniture. The business owner is a descendent of the people who founded Ephrata Cloister in Pennsylvania, an early seventeenth-century settlement based on a German Protestant monastic model. They are mainly known for the Cloister Press, which produced books and tracts with ornately beautiful lettering embellished in color by artists, and that's the main art we follow today. However, in a smaller way, Ephrata furniture's simple designs and careful, quality workmanship are also in some demand, especially by those favoring today's modern designs. That's my department. I'm glad to say that good quality does sell, and we have a relatively busy showroom. We also make furniture to order."

Carrie said, "Oh, I love that idea. Are you close enough that I could visit?"

"Probably. Eureka Springs."

"We were married there, in the Crescent Hotel," Carrie said. She looked at Henry. "We will definitely plan a trip soon."

Levi leaned forward, put his elbows on his knees, and looked down at the floor. "Not sure how soon I will get back," he said. "And, I'm sorry about that. I love my work and the lovely open surroundings there." He looked up, his eyes seeking first Carrie's face, then Henry's. "I love open areas. When I was a child, my father often locked me in a closet for disobedience to his rules. Blackness." He shuddered visibly. "Since then I have never been good with enclosed places. Marie's and my home has mainly open areas, and, instead of closets, I designed shelves and racks for storage of clothing, some of them behind cabinet doors. We also use furniture with drawers, of course."

"Oh, yes, I understand," Henry said.

After another awkward silence, he continued, changing the subject. "You said monastic. Ephrata believers were celibate?"

"Yes. There were orders for both sisters and brothers, and they were kept entirely separate, to the degree that the brothers cooked their own meals, and the sisters cut wood for their fires."

"Woo," said Carrie. "So, I assume Ephrata Cloister didn't last long."

"It had pretty much died out by 1800. However, there was also a married order of believers who lived outside the cloister itself. Our business owner is, of course, descended from that order."

"Very interesting," she said. "I am eager to visit your workplace."

"Sonita has a book about Ephrata," Levi said. "I am sure she'd be glad to loan it to you."

"Lunch is ready," Marie said from the doorway.

* * *

As they were driving home, conversation was about the good lunch Marie had prepared and about baby Summer, who stayed silent when she was brought in for all to admire. But, as soon as they were inside the house, Carrie stopped walking and turned toward Henry. "Are you thinking what I'm thinking?" she asked.

"That Marie and Levi are probably the missing couple Tracker was searching for?"

"Yes. Am I dreaming?"

"Not at all. In fact, I agree fully. I don't know exactly how they worked it all out, but, after they left our house, they could have hiked up the hill, got in their own car, which was waiting there, and drove it into the garage. Maybe it's a small thing, but another affirmation is that he's reluctant to be seen publicly. For example, why couldn't he go into town himself to pick out and load his lumber? The size of the pieces he ordered would have gone easily in his car, and normally someone so careful about quality would have wanted to approve of the quality of the wood he was buying. Then, there's the problem about small, confined places—like a jail cell."

"I thought of that, too. So, what are we going to do?"

"Nothing. Absolutely nothing."

Carrie smiled up at Henry, and said, "Do you think Sonita, and maybe Will, know?"

"One of them would have had to help get Marie and Levi's car to their road. But Carrie, we know nothing for sure, and that's okay." He smiled down at her. "This case is closed."

Then, standing together in front of their coat closet, Carrie and Henry stretched out their arms for a hug that would seal the vow of silence they had just made.

WHAT DID THE SCARECROW HEAR?

"Halloween in two weeks," Henry said. "We haven't missed a Halloween visit to Ozark Folk Center State Park since we were married."

Carrie burst out laughing. "Henry, this is the first Halloween that's come up since we were married."

"Well, there was the time we helped save Dulcie Mason and roomed together, celibately, of course. That was near Halloween. Then last year we went to visit the Masons and helped Margaret Culpepper celebrate her hundred and first birthday. That was Halloween. We were almost married, then."

"All right. But if you're talking about a visit this year, with all that's been going on here, I forgot about Halloween at the Folk Center, and that makes me very unhappy now. How could I have done that? But it's probably too late to get reservations. Come to think of it, last year I promised Pumpkin Jean I'd be back for a Halloween visit if she'd let me take over for her in the scarecrow outfit for part of a day. I need to email her to tell her I can't be there."

"Oh," Henry said, a little too smugly, "I've had our reservations since last August." Then he laughed, ducking quickly when she tossed the dish cloth in his direction.

And missed.

SPLAT.

* * *

Carrie couldn't hug her friend Pumpkin Jean when they met at the Folk Center on the morning before Halloween, because Jean had her huge pumpkin head on, along with the scarecrow outfit that went with it.

"Carrie McCrite, am I glad to see you," Jean said. "I remembered your promise from last year to sit in for me this year, and Edward and I have tentatively planned a day trip to visit our son and his family in Blytheville tomorrow. Are you still willing to take my place? But maybe a whole day is too much, and..."

"Oh, I'd love it, Jean. But you'll have to show me the ropes. And, how about Maggie? I know you usually visit her at the carousel a couple of times each day. Do you have alfalfa treats ready for me to take to her, and will she accept them from me?"

"Honey, she will accept those treats from anyone. I really don't approve of that, but heck, who can train a donkey to be sensible?

"Now, first lesson. Can you put on all this stuff and sit absolutely motionless if there are any visitors in the area? It is tough, but the whole point is fooling visitors into thinking you are simply a hay-stuffed scarecrow with a papier mache pumpkin head on top and then startling them when you lift your hand as they reach over to grab candy from your basket."

"I can do it, I promise," Carrie said. "I've watched you enough that I think I have the system figured out. Oh, Jean, I am so excited. When should I arrive in the morning?"

"How about 8:00? Henry can help you dress in the gift shop storage room and get you settled on the porch with the candy basket and alfalfa cubes. Stay out as long as you like. Close down time is 5:00 at the latest, which is when Halloween festivities in the parking lot and up here on the outdoor performance stage begin. Actually, you'll need to stop just a bit before 5:00 so you can get back in the gift shop storage room to change into your street clothes.

"I always sit with Edward in his truck while I eat lunch. When there's a quiet time, I sometimes take bathroom breaks, leaving the pumpkin head on the Gift Shop manager's desk. Don't worry about using the bathroom. These overalls have an elastic pull down in back like kids' onesie pajamas. I had them made especially. Otherwise a bathroom break would take an hour or more."

Jean began laughing. "Oh, Carrie, I am so excited about this, and I can't thank you enough."

"Well, I hope I do okay. In any case, it will be fun."

Jean lifted off her pumpkin head, which startled a couple heading for the candle shop, and said, "Okay, let's go to the storage room so I can show you my system and give pointers about how to get into this costume. Is Henry with you?"

"Yes. We're married now, you know."

"Whoopie. Well, that's great.

"Okay. Lesson One. See these bales of hay I have my feet propped on? Henry can pull out some strands from the ends and stick them in your sleeves and the overall's legs. That helps with the scarecrow illusion. Hay can be prickly, though, so you'll have to guide him in arranging it. It's a good idea to have on heavy underwear, at least on your legs, since sometimes the hay can prickle, even through the overall fabric. Oh, gosh, I hope you have heavy underwear with you. It can get chilly, sitting still out here."

When Carrie nodded, Jean said, "Okay, come with me for your lesson."

* * *

The next morning, Carrie, dressed in Jean's worn flannel shirt, overalls, and boots, clumped out to the Gift Shop porch carrying the candy basket, while Henry carried the pumpkin head and bag of alfalfa cubes. When Carrie was settled on the bench with her feet and legs propped on hay bales and bits of hay sticking out over her gloved hands and Jean's well-worn boots, he lowered the large papier mache pumpkin over her head and rested it on her shoulders.

"How's that?"

"Swivel it a bit to the right so I can see people coming out the gift shop door through the eye holes. Okay, that's good. Now, tuck the bag of alfalfa cubes behind my left leg, and place the candy basket here, on my lap."

He took a caramel from the basket after he'd put it on her lap. "Is that placement okay?"

She tried to nod, discovered she couldn't, and said, "Yes, it's okay." Then she said, "Uh, Henry—Jean called. She said she might be late getting back tomorrow morning, so asked if I'd be able to sit in for a while then. I said I would."

"Okay with me." He unwrapped the candy and popped it in his mouth. "Hmm, wooks wike you have about every bwand of candy known to concession stands in movie theatres. This caramel is good. Wonder where she gets them?"

"You'll have to ask. But, before you leave, I saw there weren't many caramels, so put a caramel here in my pocket. I'll eat it later."

"What happens if folks eat all your candy?"

"Jean said Gift Shop employees check on that and refill if necessary." She skootched one leg a tiny bit. "Okay, I guess I'm settled. Do you want to sit over there on the wall for a bit and see if I manage this caper as well as Jean did?"

"Oh, I'm sure you will, though I assume sitting still for so long will be your biggest challenge. Okay, I'll watch for a bit. Then I'm off to the Wood Shop. Clarence promised to show me how he cuts out and shapes his wooden pull toys. And, after we have lunch, I will probably spend the afternoon at the blacksmith's forge. I want to see if I can help Howdy make a couple of trivets for our wood stove while we're here."

"Howdy?"

"Short for Howard. Sort of. And I will try to come back and check on you at least every hour."

"Okay. And you should call me 'Pumpkin Jean.' Jean never did say if folks here knew someone was taking over for her today."

"Well, you look just like she did, so it really doesn't matter." He went to sit on the stone wall across from the Gift Shop porch.

Carrie caught her first visitor only a few minutes later. A family with three children came to watch the top maker and, while the two younger children stared, wide-eyed, at the spinning foot-powered lathe, an older boy turned and walked over to look at Pumpkin Jean. He poked at Carrie's leg, which tested her ability to stay quiet, then spread his fingers and started to take a large handful of candy. "Hey" she growled, Jean style, extending her gloved hand like a lightning bolt and pulling the candy basket out of his reach. "One to a customer."

He dropped the candy in the basket and jumped back. "You're real!"

"You betcha. And now you can count out five pieces to share with your family, with one for yourself."

"O-oh kay. Uh, thank you." He counted pieces carefully and went to join his family where, both Carrie and Henry noticed, gestures and looks back at the Pumpkin Lady meant he was explaining that she was a real person.

After a few more minutes and two ordinary visitors who simply took one piece of candy each without paying much attention to who held the basket, Henry stood, formed his fingers into the "OK" gesture, smiled and nodded at Carrie, then left for the Wood Shop.

After that there was a steady stream of people all morning, which meant a Gift Shop worker had to come out twice to refill the basket, and, other than small shifts in posture to ease bored muscles, Carrie had no problem with staying quiet enough to fool most visitors.

Lunch with Henry went just fine, but, after a quick bathroom break, she hurried back to the Gift Shop porch. "This is loads of fun," she told Henry, as he helped her get resettled on the bench and hay bales. "So much is going on that I don't get bored. And you should see folks' reactions when I move my hand!"

There was a quiet time after she went back to work, and she assumed most Folk Center visitors were eating lunch at the nearby Smoke House Snack Bar or in the Iron Skillet Restaurant. During one quiet period, a couple of men came out of the gift shop and stood near her bench. The one wearing a tan windbreaker carried a large tote bag holding something heavy. They both looked around before the man in the blue pullover said, "Did you check out the area?" Though the sentence was simple, his tone said Tan Jacket would be sorry if he hadn't checked whatever area was meant.

"I checked. The plan is good. They always put the donkey that pulls the carousel in that fenced pasture for the night. No one stays nearby."

Both men looked around again, fidgeted, then paced a few steps to the left of Carrie. She could no longer see them through the eye slits in her pumpkin head and heard only bits of their conversation through her pumpkin-covered ears.

"...dark....get in?" It was Blue Sweater's voice.

"Easy...hide." That was Tan Jacket. "Lift hook."

Mumbling, then "...kick me?" A laugh from Blue Sweater, and more words she couldn't hear.

Tan Jacket laughed too. "No chance! Look, got this..."

The sack rustled. Carrie wished she dared move her head to see what was in the sack.

"Great. That'll do the trick." The rustling stopped as both men laughed again, and moved back in front of Carrie, pausing so close that Tan Jacket's jeans were almost brushing her foot as he said, "Unless you need me this afternoon I'm gonna walk back to the RV to take a nap. People putting stuff in that metal dumpster kept me awake last night. I don't know how you slept through it all."

"The sleep of the innocent. You go on. I don't plan to say anything about you being here anyway. I'll tell him I've unlocked the gate and say I picked the donkey carousel area because it's closed at night, making it a safe place for the two of us to meet without being seen or bothered. We'll have plenty of time to agree on our business deal and for me to get his payment. Then you can come in and..." Blue Sweater laughed again. "Don't oversleep. Meet me as arranged. Dress plain, all dark colors."

"You don't need to tell me," Tan Jacket said. "Hey, look, there's real candy in the scarecrow's basket."

This time Pumpkin Jean-Carrie did not reach out to grab her victim, even though he took several candy bars. In fact, to be sure the illusion held, she almost stopped breathing until he stepped back.

"Let's go, people are coming," Tan Jacket said, dropping a candy wrapper near the hay bales.

Carrie thought about the two men between visitors all afternoon. What had that peculiar conversation meant? Surely she should tell someone what she'd overheard! A couple of times she even forgot to grab her victims.

Finally, as 4:00 neared, Carrie slid off the bench.

She waited a few moments for everything making up her personal meat and bones to unkink, then lifted off the pumpkin head. Moving clumsily in the heavy boots, she trudged toward the storage room to change clothes. She'd decided to quit early so she would have time to tell someone in administration what she'd overheard.

Thirty minutes later she left the administration building, wondering whether to be miffed or relieved. No one there had sounded patronizing, but they didn't sound alarmed either. She didn't reveal that she had seen and overheard the men while disguised as Pumpkin Jean, which, she thought, didn't matter since, out in the open, she could have seen and heard them more clearly. But, to folks in Admin, she was just one more tourist.

The director said, "Maybe they were workmen of some kind. I'll ask around. And a park ranger is on patrol every night. He checks the entire Crafts Village during his patrol. He'll be sure nothing happens.

"Thanks for telling us what you heard. Believe me, we really appreciate your concern."

* * *

Carrie was barely settled on her bench the next morning when a stir, then an outright ruckus, came from the upper level of the Crafts Village. The sounds seemed to be centered beyond the auditorium, probably somewhere near the carousel and donkey yard.

Those men had mentioned the donkey yard. Maggie!

Just then Clive, Maggie's handler hurried up to her and said, "Jean, come quick, there's big trouble in Maggie's pasture."

Before she could explain who she was, he had hurried away so, leaving her pumpkin head on the Gift Shop manager's desk, she hurried after him. When she heard Maggie braying loudly, her concern wavered. Surely the donkey was all right if she could make that much noise.

But, when she reached the pasture, anxiety returned full force.

Clive and Maggie were standing next to the fence at the farthest distance from a man lying on the ground near the pasture gate. There was blood on his head.

"Oh, please, no," Carrie thought, not realizing she had spoken the words aloud as she opened the pasture gate.

One of the park rangers in the group kneeling by the man looked up at her. "Stay back. We've called an ambulance."

"Is he...?" She couldn't say the word.

Just then the man moaned and moved one of his legs, answering her unfinished question. A ranger took off his jacket and covered the injured man's chest and arms.

Feeling numb, as if she were dreaming, Carrie went to Maggie and began stroking her neck. The donkey nuzzled her pocket, looking for a treat. Without thinking, Carrie pulled out her caramel and gave it to Maggie, wrapper and all.

"Where's Jean?" The donkey handler whispered.

After she'd explained, he said, still whispering, "They say Maggie did that." He used his elbow to point to the man on the ground.

"They say WHAT?" She forgot to whisper, but no one near the fallen man looked up.

Maggie drooled caramel, then stamped a hoof next to Carrie's boot.

"Sorry, girl," Carrie said, "I forgot the alfalfa cubes. I'll bring a real treat later."

"They say she attacked him. They say she kicked him because he was bothering her, maybe trying to steal her. The ranger on patrol says he didn't hear any noises, but look." He removed his hand from the rope that was holding Maggie and pointed. "The gate to the auditorium parking lot isn't hooked. They think this man, and maybe another, drove up with a horse trailer during the night and got the gate open somehow. Coulda even taken the inside hook off before the park closed." He shook his head. "I maybe forgot to check it before I left."

"Phooey. Seems to me the ranger on patrol could not have missed seeing a horse trailer and the truck that brought it, assuming he wasn't taking a nap. Wouldn't trying to load her have taken quite a bit of time and made a lot of noise? She probably would have raised a ruckus that could have been heard all over this park. I've spent quite a bit of time here, and I'm good friends with Jean, so I've gotten to know Maggie too. I've never known her to be the quiet type. But she is very gentle. When she's in harness ready to pull the carousel around, she lets the children pet her. Sometimes they even poke or swat. I've never seen her react to any of that."

She stopped stroking Maggie's neck and walked toward the group huddled around the injured man.

A sad-eyed ranger stopped her. "You don't want to look at this," he said. "The man's hurt bad. And since that donkey has started attacking people, she's going to have to be removed."

"Nonsense," Carrie said as she pushed past him and bent down near the man's head.

The ranger kneeling there said, "Stop right there,

lady. I don't know who you are, but..."

"Jean left Maggie as my responsibility since she had to be away for a while. So, show me what you're looking at."

The ranger glanced at her for a moment, noticing the scarecrow costume. Then he said, "The man must have been stupid enough to bend over behind the donkey. You can see the animal's hoof imprint on him more than once. Down here near his chin there's no blood, but if you look close, you'll see the print of a horseshoe."

"Ah, yes I do see. Clive, lift up one of Maggie's hooves so these men can see the bottom of it."

Clive lifted, without objection from Maggie. The men looked.

"Clive, has Maggie ever worn horseshoes?"

"Nope, donkeys have strong hooves. She's never been shod."

Hubbub. Questions and much discussion. Then the ambulance came, the injured man was taken away, and everyone left, except for a ranger who would stay on guard until detectives got there to search the pasture for clues. Maggie, placid through all this, was fed several alfalfa cubes and taken out into the Crafts Village where Clive tied her next to the sheep and goats.

In the meantime, fortified by a sandwich Henry brought from the Smoke House, Carrie waited in a police car to be interviewed. Henry sat in the back seat, more or less, Carrie thought, as if he were on guard while she was questioned.

The young officer who came seemed more inclined to talk than listen, but she noticed he did at least make notes while she described Blue Sweater and Tan Jacket.

"Is there anything more you can recall about those two men you overheard on the Gift Shop porch?"

"Let me get my thoughts in order," she said.

She shut her eyes, picturing what she had seen and heard. "They came out of the Gift Shop. First, Blue Sweater asked Tan Jacket if he had checked the area. From what was said then, I could tell he meant the carousel area. Then someone said the donkey would be in the pasture at night, and Blue Sweater said something about 'kick me.'

"Tan Jacket was carrying a sack with something heavy in it, and both he and Blue Sweater looked at it, though I couldn't see what it was."

Henry interrupted. "Excuse me. I was in the Blacksmith Shop all afternoon. I didn't see these men while I was there, but given the marks on the injured man, I wonder if they didn't buy one of the tools with real horseshoe handles. They could have used that to injure the man found on the ground."

"Yes," Carrie said, "I bet that's it. Well, from what was said, it was obvious that Blue Sweater planned to meet someone in Maggie's pasture. Money and some kind of business deal were mentioned. Then Tan Jacket said he was going to the RV to take a nap, since folks putting trash in the metal dumpster near where they were parked kept him awake all night. Blue Sweater said he planned to meet the visitor alone anyway and told Tan Jacket to wear something dark and then—well I don't know what then."

The officer, still writing, said, "Blue and Tan probably intended to kill that man since he could identify Blue at least. We'll notify the state police and other law enforcement offices to be on the watch for them. I wonder which park that RV was in. Possibly folks at that office can describe their rig."

"Wait a minute!" Carrie said. "Since both men were on foot, I'd bet they were located in the park right here, next to the Folk Center. And, you know what, they could still be there. They would feel no concern about being discovered if you're right and they intended to kill the only person who can identify at least one of them. They seemed pretty laid back about what they planned to do and probably think that man is dead."

"Right. The RV next to the dumpster," the police officer said.

Carrie and Henry opened car doors and barely had time to get out of the way of the police car before it roared off.

"Well, that's that," Carrie said. "I'm going back to get my pumpkin head. I want to enjoy at least a few more minutes of 'Catch the candy grabber' before Jean comes to take over. Why don't you go make another trivet? This time, how about making one out of a horseshoe?"

THE TATTLE-TALE

"I think I'll head to Penney's this morning. I'd like to find a new pair of navy slacks and, according to the newspaper, they're having a good sale. Do you want to come along?" Carrie chuckled before she continued. "Need any socks or underwear?"

Henry looked up from the lamp he was repairing. "Umm, don't think so. Besides, I have a list of small household chores to take care of today. You go on."

An hour and a half later, Carrie was sitting on the bench in a dressing room trying to decide which of two pairs of slacks she liked best. Since the area was totally quiet, she felt no guilt about taking extra time to debate with herself about which to choose. The other dressing rooms were obviously empty.

Well—why not buy both? That would solve the problem, and, after all, the sale price made buying two not much more expensive than one would have been at the original price.

Satisfied with her decision, she stood, put the slacks over her arm, and was about to open the door when voices announced that a mother and child had chosen the dressing room next to hers. The child's voice said, "Momma, did I do good? You said if I knocked over that watch display the lady would come to help me pick things up, since you told her you couldn't bend because of my baby sister in your tummy. But, why isn't pushing over displays naughty?"

"Never mind. We needed to see if she was a good clerk, that's all. Now, take your sweater off. I want you to put this red one on."

"I like my blue sweater."

"We'll put it back on over the red one. I'll help, hold your arms up."

Staying quiet, Carrie sat down again. *What on earth?*

"Don't want another sweater. Too hot."

"Hush."

"HOT, Momma."

"I said hush! Do what I say. Don't you like this red sweater?"

"Yes, but if you carry it to the counter, won't they put it in a sack?"

"I want you to wear it. Put it on now, or I'll smack you."

Silence. Rustling.

"Okay, now let's put your old sweater on over the new one. You can take it off in the car if you're still hot. Do what I say. Lift your arms."

More silence. Then the child's voice said, "You gonna put that dress in with my baby sister?"

"What baby sister? Oh, yes, I just told the lady that for fun. I want to try the dress on at home and see if it goes with my green shoes. If it does, I'll come back and pay for it."

"If my baby sister is in there, won't the dress hurt her? And, since that extra tummy opens up, why can't she come out now?"

"There is no baby sister. I only said that for fun. Now turn around. I need to put some things in your backpack."

"Why?"

"So, we can take them home to try. I'll bring them back if we don't like them."

"That's a pretty bracelet. You gonna see if you like that, too?"

"Yes. Now, no more talking. We'll hurry to the car. Do not talk when we are out in the store. Do you understand me?"

Carrie sat very still on the bench. *Oh, my, oh, my. What should I do?*

There was a brief, whiny-sounding noise from the

child, then the dressing room door opened and shut, and all was silent.

Carrie's mind raced wildly as she stood. If she reported what she'd heard and the mother was charged with theft, what would happen to that child? But, if she didn't report it and the shoplifting continued while the mother used the child as cover, what then?

Finally, coming to a conclusion, she left the dressing room.

The mother and child were approaching the exit doors when she caught up with them. The mother released her hold on the girl and was using both hands to push through the first door when Carrie dropped her slacks on the floor in front of the child, who now lagged behind.

"Oops," she said and, stooping down to pick them up, came face-to-face with a small, wide-eyed girl wearing a blue sweater and a pink backpack.

"What a pretty sweater," Carrie said as the mother stopped, put both hands on her baby bulge, and turned back toward them. The girl pulled up the front of her blue sweater to show the edge of a red sweater underneath. She grinned as she held up two fingers.

"Oh, I bet that red sweater will be nice for you to

wear next Christmas. I'd like to see more of it. May I?" The child lifted the front of the blue sweater, revealing the front of a red sweater with a tag hanging from a seam on the side.

Momma arrived and grabbed her daughter by the arm, starting to yank her away.

Carrie, just as quickly, took hold of the child's backpack by the top of its Velcro-fastened pocket. Out popped several pieces of jewelry, attracting the attention of a worker who was wheeling a loaded dress display rack along the aisle.

Carrie yelled, "Call Security!"

"You little thief, what have you done?" Momma slapped her daughter and began raging at her in terms that shouldn't be said to anyone, let alone a child. She went through the exit door, pulling her daughter with her, while Carrie hurried after them, shouting as loudly as she could, "Wait, wait, you forgot something." The mother hesitated and looked back toward Carrie.

It was enough time. A sturdy male in uniform came to the exit, caught up with the fleeing woman, put a hand on each of her arms, and urged her back inside. Carrie, after a nod from the man, put an arm around the child, who, as she began to cry, said, "Momma, I didn't talk in the store."

What was Henry going to say? This could mean a court appearance. Ah, well, she was still sure she had made the right decision.

* * *

Dear Reader,

If you were in Carrie's place, what decision would you have made?

A DANGEROUS DANCE

Carrie was involved with the washer and dryer when Henry appeared in the laundry room door. She looked up at him, but he said nothing until she had finished transferring jeans from washer to dryer. Then he said, "Ray called."

"Ray?"

"Yes, Ray. Surely you haven't forgotten Deputy Police Chief Rayford Duncan, my buddy and one-time partner in Kansas City. You know—Ray and his wife Rose."

"Oh, of course! I guess his interesting full name, Rayford, was stuck in my head. Ray and Rose and her recipe for 'Mama's Saucy Hamburger.' Come to think of it, we haven't made that for a while. It's time we did.

"Rose and I got on so well. Y'know, we did promise we'd come back to Kansas City to visit them, and we haven't. They were so kind to us when we got into that mess about the theft of the emerald, and...oh, did he share news? Is everything okay there? Surely..."

For a minute Henry looked at her in silence, then he chuckled and said, "I was beginning to wonder when you'd ask why he called."

"Sorry, I was babbling. So, Mr. Police Major Detective Henry King, why did Ray call?"

"Ah, ha. The Policeman's—oh, I mean Police Officer's ball—is coming up next month, and he invited us to come. He said we could stay at their home, which, he explained quite seriously, would be okay, since their neighborhood has a few white families and we pale faces wouldn't stand out too much. I said I was sure we'd be very pleased to come, but that I'd check with you and call him back to confirm and make final arrangements. How about it? I'll warn you, it's veddy, veddy formal—tuxedo or full-dress uniform and ball gowns. It's okay if you say, 'I haven't a thing to wear.' We can go shopping for your ball gown, beginning this afternoon, if that's okay. No time like the present. Ray said Rose is wearing an autumn-leaf rust color, full-length gown, and I want a commendation for thinking to ask about that."

"Oh, for heaven's sake, okay, you are commended, and I am very glad Ray invited us to come.

Any special reason?"

"He did mention something about a commendation, so I guess he's getting an acknowledgement for service from the department, the mayor, or some group. Whatever it is, he deserves it."

"I sure enjoyed being with them last summer. Autumn leaf color, hm? That will be beautiful with Rose's brown skin tones. I'm already excited about this, mostly for the chance to spend time with Ray and Rose, but there's no need to go shopping. I already have something to wear. My wedding dress will be just fine."

"Oh, no, we'll buy you a proper ball gown."

"Why can't I wear my wedding dress? No one in Kansas City has seen it."

"Because I want to help you pick out a beautiful gown. And, you can get one with..." He used his finger to draw a low curve on his chest. "What is the word? Cleavage." He walked up to her and put a finger against her shirt. "Down to here, showing a bit of what Shirley calls bazooms."

"Henry King, you've seen me naked and you know quite well my front is no longer suited for cleavage."

"We'll see, we'll see. Now, how about this afternoon? We can start at that place in the mall with the windows full of fancy dresses for brides and women attending other formal occasions. I can tell from their displays they might have something that we—I said WE—will like."

"So, you've been looking at those display dresses, have you? Hmm. No wonder you said 'cleavage,' but I am shocked you even knew the word."

"My dear wife, I am a man of many mysteries."

Their laughter was eventually quieted by a heated embrace. It wasn't until later that Carrie remembered Henry's first wife, Irena, had been from a wealthy Kansas City family and undoubtedly owned a closet full of ball gowns.

Still, she was surprised when Henry walked confidently into "Your Perfect Gown" and, ignoring a bride-to-be wearing a dress that most certainly showed a lot of cleavage, approached a clerk young enough to be his granddaughter. "We'd like to look at your selection of ball gowns. My wife and I are attending the Police Officer's Ball in Kansas City next month, and she needs a proper dress. I came along to enjoy watching her choose a gown and, where appropriate, give my opinion. We like that pink one in the window, but..."

Carrie interrupted, "But I am not a pink person, and the neckline on that dress is quite low. Not suitable for my mature figure. May we look at other selections?"

"Of course, and we can certainly find the perfect gown for you. Let's go to one of our comfortable viewing rooms where your husband can watch you try on our gowns in private. I'm Chloe," she said, looking at Carrie, then up at Henry. "I will be glad to bring a selection of dresses for you to see, Ms..."

"I'm Carrie, and this is Henry," Carrie said, winking at him as the clerk led them toward a white and gold door.

Chloe pulled out a tape measure as soon as they were in the room and Henry was seated in an armchair upholstered in what looked like white leather. "Now, let's check measurements, though the timing will give us an opportunity for any needed garment adjustments. What colors do you like, Carrie?"

"Blue, aqua, teal. I think ivory and white will look too bridish, and I am not fond of green, purple, or lavender."

"Red?" Chloe asked.

"Oh, my, no. I used to be a red head and never wore..."

"Yes," Henry said. "Red is also a possibility."

"No," Carrie said. "I'd clash with Rose."

* * *

The array of rejected dresses with demure neck-
lines had become almost bewildering by the time
Chloe wheeled in a rack with two dresses, one red,
one burgundy.

"Maybe the burgundy," Carrie said wearily, then
started to tell Chloe not to bother when she saw the
neckline.

"Beautiful fabric," Henry said. "Would you call
it brocade? Is it heavy? Carrie has to be free to dance
the night away."

"Why don't you take it off the rack and hand it
to your wife?"

"Oh, not heavy at all. Uh, here, Carrie."

Chloe took over and slipped the gown over
Carrie's now flying wild white curls. "Look there,
perfect fit."

"But the neckline, I'm just not..."

"I'll be right back," Chloe said. "Would you slip
out of the dress top and take off your bra while I'm
gone?"

Carrie, too startled to reply in time, obeyed and,
for some reason, felt horribly embarrassed when she
saw Henry looking at her and smiling.

Chloe came back with two items that Carrie could
not identify. "This is what we call a bosom-shaper

cami," she said, helping Carrie put on something that looked like one of her winter underwear tops. Except, except...

The clerk was gently urging Carrie's breasts into soft padded pockets on the cami. "Now, do you see how I did that? Comfortable? Okay, dress top back up."

Carrie stared in the mirror. "I, uh...oh, my."

The second item was a large lace collar in a slightly lighter burgundy color than the dress fabric. It went over Carrie's head and floated onto the dress top, shadowing, but not hiding the—

"Cleavage," Henry said, then added, "it is beautiful, and Carrie is beautiful in it. Okay, my dear? Thank you, Chloe. We will take this gown and the two items you brought in to go with it. May we please have the dress on a hanger?"

Carrie was way beyond any ability to comment and just nodded.

* * *

Rose insisted on beginning to dress for the ball early, and it wasn't long before Carrie understood why. She hadn't been a girly-chatterer even when a girl, but now she and Rose helped each other into their gowns with a lot of interruptions for laughing, shifting, arranging, and zipping. They both giggled almost constantly, and Carrie didn't even bother to be embarrassed when she showed the mysteries of the bosom shaper to Rose, who studied the arrangement carefully.

"Oh, girl," Rose said, "wish I needed one of those. There's too much of me, so I need a reducer, not a shaper."

Looking at Rose's exuberant cleavage, Carrie said, "I'm sure Ray approves of cleavage, which, I learned, is quite stylish these days. Henry certainly approved it for this new dress."

"Men," Rose said, as they finished checking make-up and hair in the mirror and walked out to greet waiting husbands who, of course, had been fully dressed for some time.

* * *

The hotel ballroom was awesome, but people-watching was, for Carrie, even more so. She wondered if Kansas City's male police officers were required to be handsome and the women—whether they were officers, wives, or girlfriends—to be beautiful. *Guess the atmosphere and occasion, and even the subdued lighting, have something to do with it,* she thought, as Henry put a possessive arm around her and an usher guided the four of them to a reserved table at the front.

"Oh, my goodness," she said, as they stepped up to the platform holding their table. "The head table? I sure didn't expect this. You should have warned me."

"Couldn't," Henry said. "Didn't know myself until Ray told me while we were waiting for you girls to get dressed. By the way, what was all the giggling about?"

"You'll never know," she said.

"Well, none-the-less, you must admit the wedding dress would not have done. Now you look like a queen—my queen," he added, as a server put plates of a complicated-looking salad in front of them.

After the meal there were, of course, speeches. Eventually Ray said, "We have a special honor to give tonight, and I have a special interest in the honoree, as do several officers in this room." He turned to Henry. "To retired Police Major Henry J. King, a former homicide detective here, who, our records show, by his brave actions and quick thinking, saved the lives of more of our officers, including my own, than anyone else in the history of this department. Please stand, Henry."

It took a minute for Henry to react, but when Carrie whispered, "Get up now," he did.

"This is only an inadequate commendation in the

face of lives saved, but it is one way for us to say, 'Thank you,'" Ray said, as he took a medal from its box and pinned it on Henry's jacket. He then handed Henry an engraved plaque, and said, "May this be an encouraging beacon for all our officers as we work together through the years, and the sometimes tough, dangerous challenges we face."

Henry looked down at Carrie for a moment, looked back at Ray and then the audience. "I...well, it didn't seem so special at those times. Don't we all look out for each other? Isn't that part of our code of ethics, or at least our gut feeling? Any one of you would have done the same for me. As for you female officers, in the past we've had too few of you, and I was never partnered with a woman. Until now—my wife, Carrie." As the applause and whistling began, Henry reached down and pulled her to her feet.

Yes, thank goodness he insisted on a new dress, she thought.

* * *

Finally, it was time to dance. If she and Henry held each other a bit more tightly than made dancing easy, probably others understood.

After three dances they went to the side of the room and sat in chairs provided there. Carrie said, "Be right back, going to the Ladies." Henry stood when she did, and then, she was sure, watched her all the way to the exit door before he sat down again.

As she left the restroom, a woman in the starched white coat of a restaurant chef hurried up and, taking a firm hold on her arm, said, "Something has happened, and Henry needs you. Come with me."

Carrie's initial heart thud was followed by a momentary mental blankness, then a quick appeal to God followed by a burning alertness. Who was this woman? There were police officers aplenty who could alert her to any urgent need in the ballroom. *Why such a message from this woman, who was obviously from the kitchen?*

"Wait," Carrie said. "I can make it back to the ballroom on my own. I don't need your help." She tried to pull her arm out of the woman's grasp, but the hold tightened painfully.

Carrie said, "Let me go," and tried to free her arm again, but was unable to break away from the woman's strong grasp. "Why are you doing this?" she asked. "I assume Henry does not need me after all, and I don't know you. My husband and I are not wealthy, so I don't think kidnapping is the reason, and I'm sure I've never done anything to harm you. Why, then?"

They had turned away from the restroom area

into a narrow, dark hallway, and, as they entered it, a door to one of the rooms along the side opened, and a young man in a sweatshirt and jeans appeared. "Ah, Mom, I see you brought the lady." He put a hand around Carrie's free arm but held on gently as his mother began pulling her along the hall, and Carrie yelled, "Help! Help!"

The woman laughed. "This whole area is sound-proofed to protect folks in the ballroom from hearing kitchen noises, so yell all you want."

Carrie stopped yelling and concentrated on thinking and praying.

"Why are you doing this?" she finally asked. "I have no idea who you are. I've never seen either of you before."

"But Police Officer Henry King has. He arrested my son Mikey twenty years ago and got him sent to prison. Mikey was murdered there last month. So, when I heard your husband's name on the public address and he mentioned you, I thought, now's the time to show Henry King what it's like to lose someone you love. I went out, pretending to be checking on the removal of used dishes and got a good look at you. Then I called Jerry. He's Mikey's brother. Never been involved with cops and has a good job, but of course he hated what happened to

Mikey, and he agreed to come help me. All I had to do was keep an eye on the restroom hallway. Most women at a banquet eventually come there, so I was sure you would."

Carrie wondered if she dared ask why Mikey was sent to prison and decided against it. She said, "Oh, no, I am so sorry. I am sure Henry did not mean for your Mikey to die."

There was no answer. The three of them stopped at a closed door. The woman opened it while Jerry held both of Carrie's arms and guided her inside the room. When the light was turned on, she saw that this room was not an office, but a storage area. Several chairs matching what they had used at the banquet were there, and Carrie was pushed down in one of them. Jerry produced two men's ties. "You said to bring ties, so I grabbed these."

"Real ties? Oh, for blank sake, Jerry. Those were your dad's ties. You shouldna' bothered them."

"Well, you said ties, what was I to think?"

"Oh, never mind. Guess that's all we have now to tie her up. Do her feet first."

The woman took over holding her arms while Jerry crouched down by her feet. When it was obvious he was going to tie her to the chair, Carrie started to lift a foot to kick him but decided it would be best to avoid doing anything to make him angry. One tie went around her ankles, was woven through the chair's decorative underbracing, and knotted. He then went behind the chair, moved his mother aside, and took hold of Carrie's arms. As he tried to pull them together toward the center back, she yelped and said, "Oh, please, you about broke my arm."

"Tie's not long enough to get both hands tied back here, Mom."

"Tie her wrists together. I'll bring kitchen towels we can rip up for ties after I write a note to Officer King."

She reached under her white jacket and pulled out a large kitchen knife. "Here, you stand behind her and hold the knife against her neck while I go fix the note and get it to him. I have a plan so he won't know where it came from. Don't hurt her now unless she tries to fight."

Carrie heard the bolt turn after the woman left the room. So! Both she and Jerry were prisoners. Maybe she could make something of that with Jerry.

Her thoughts had been totally involved in thinking about God being there with her, and that seemed to be more sensible than trying to think of how she could escape from these people. When Jerry's hand shook as he held the knife at what she would call a completely safe distance from her throat, she wondered if he was totally committed to what was going on or just doing what his mother said.

With some surprise her thoughts suddenly settled on the idea that, if we are all God's children—as she often said to pupils in her Sunday School class—that meant Jerry and his mother were included, though they weren't acting like it now. Still, the woman's actions could be the result of grief because her son had been killed. She had said 'murdered.' How awful!

Eventually Carrie said, "I am very sorry about your brother, but I don't want you to get involved in anything illegal because of his death. I am sure you mean no harm to me, nor does your mother."

"Shut up," he said.

* * *

Henry located Ray and Rose on the dance floor and hurried over to them.

"Whoa, buddy, you can't cut in. Go dance with your own wife. This woman is taken."

"Rose, Carrie went to the restroom a long time ago and she should have been back by now, even if she stopped to chat with some of the women there. I thought maybe you could check and see what the delay is."

"Oh, sure," Rose said. "Ray, you sit with Henry

on the side over there."

When Rose returned, she looked worried. "Carrie isn't back there anywhere, and none of the women in the restroom remembered seeing a white-haired lady in a burgundy dress, so she must have been gone for several minutes.

"I checked the area. The restroom is in a hall near the kitchen. Another, smaller hall turns off the main one. There are three doors in that smaller hall. I tried all of them, but they were locked, and I could hear no sound inside. A door at the very end of the hall leads to the back of the hotel and had a turn knob for the lock, so I opened the door and looked out. It opens on an alley, but there was no one out there and just one car, which was empty. I saw no sign of Carrie or anyone else."

A young woman in a flaming red gown hurried up to them waving what looked like a pleated paper muffin cup. "Major King, this was around some of the snacks on a tray at the bar. No telling which of the many workers brought it."

She handed the paper to Henry, who flattened it out and read aloud, "King, my son is gone, and your wife soon will be."

Rose gasped, and there was a moment of silence before Ray said, "We'll find her, Henry, we will find her." He hurried toward the bandstand, and Henry, feeling like a robot, followed.

The music stopped, and Ray began shouting, "Folks, Police Major King's wife, Carrie, has been abducted and is possibly in danger. We need to search this floor at once. Officers Bakala, Herzog, Angelo, Markley, and Brown, find out where all the hotel's exit doors are and cover them. Get help from in here if you need it. Mosely, interview the staff on duty at the desk and ask what they remember about anyone coming through the lobby or using the elevators during the past hour. The missing woman was sitting next to Major King at the head table. She has white hair, and her dress is dark red. The rest of you, fan out to search every inch of this floor. Go in teams of two, pick a direction, and work out a grid so we cover it all. Spouses can stay here or help search, but if you leave this room, stay with your officer. A few officers should remain on guard in here. Okay, let's move!"

He turned, put his arm across Henry's back, and said, "At least we can't say we're short on staff for this. Do you want to help search or stay here?"

"Ray, that note came from the kitchen. I want to go there."

* * *

Carrie ignored Jerry's "Shut up" and asked, "Why was your brother in prison? I know my husband is not aware that he has died."

"Died last month, but him being there was a mistake. See, Mikey and some friends were driving around in Mikey's car and decided to rob a convenience store to get enough money, well, to get money for bad stuff. Mom never knew about that. The clerk there got shot, but it wasn't Mikey that shot him. He never even owned a gun, but one of the other guys did, and after he saw the clerk take out a gun from under the counter, he shot him. All three of the guys ran back to Mikey's car, and Mikey drove off. Didn't take the cops long to catch up to them since a customer coming in got the license plate number. The two guys were sitting in back, and they wiped off the gun best they could and tossed it up on the front seat next to Mikey.

"When the cops stopped them, Mikey picked up the gun and waved it around. He told me he was so scared he wasn't thinking clear and figured if the cops saw the gun, they would back off and he could drive away far enough to dump the car and run. Well, the cops didn't back off, and Mikey's fingerprints were on the gun. Besides, they'd seen him waving it around, though he said he never pointed it at them."

"So how did my husband get in that mess?"

"Oh, he was one of the cops that arrested Mikey and his friends. He saw him waving the gun. In court, he testified that Mikey had the gun and was threatening them."

"What happened to Mikey's friends?"

"They insisted Mikey was the shooter, and he kept saying he wasn't, but all three of them went to prison. At least the convenience store guy didn't die, he was just hurt bad. If he'd-a died, well, who knows? I was only twelve at the time, but even then, I didn't think the jury was for sure Mikey had been the shooter. I think that's why all three guys got the same sentence."

"How old was Mikey then?"

"Just turned seventeen."

"Juvenile, so he was only thirty-seven when he died?"

"Thirty-six. And it wasn't from being sick. He was cut by a blade somehow made there in the prison. Mikey bled to death before anyone discovered him. I'm betting it was the guy who shot the store clerk who cut him. Parole consideration was coming up, and maybe that guy thought the truth might come out. I don't know if the cops ever traced who really owned the gun, but they should have."

"Oh, Jerry, I am sorry, and I know my husband—

Officer King—will be too. This is so hard on you and your mother. I have a son about the age of your Mikey, and I know how I'd feel."

"Yeah, well, thanks. It helps that you understand. Mom just wants revenge on your husband, not you. Guess she got upset when she heard his name."

The door was yanked open and, after an instant of hope, Carrie saw that the woman in the white jacket was back. "Everything okay? She cause you any trouble?"

"No, Mom, everything is quiet here."

"I brought some kitchen towels. We'll rip them up for ties and a gag for her."

"But, if the room is soundproof, why do we need to gag her?"

"Well, maybe we don't, and we do need to hurry so you can get out of here. There's lots of activity in the banquet room, so I guess they've discovered she's missing. I didn't dare go check, but I bet they found my note."

As he began ripping the towels into strips, he said, "Mom, why didn't you figure there would be an uproar when they discovered she was missing?"

"Hey, I had to plan all this in a hurry, didn't I? I told you I only learned she and Officer King were here when I heard it on the public address during the banquet. That's when I thought I could get revenge for Mikey."

"But why take this woman? It won't help Mikey now and will just make trouble for us."

"You hush!"

"Okay, okay, calm down. I've made several towel strips. I'll work on her arms first, then I can put two strips together and tie them around her waist. So, how did you get the note to him?"

"Wrote it with a Sharpie on one of the pleated cups holding snacks that the servers took to the bar."

"Won't they know it came from the kitchen?"

"Well, maybe, but no one in there knows what I did. Could be anyone, so they'll have lots of workers and special help to interview."

"She's all secure now, Mom."

"Okay, you skedaddle then. Did you leave the TV on at home?"

"Yes. I am not stupid like..."

"Don't you call your brother stupid again."

"I didn't say that. Anyway, the neighbors will think I was home all along."

"Okay. Come back about 3:00 in the morning. Stay quiet and watch all around for a while. They'll most likely have given up on the search by then. If no one is around, you can come in, and we'll take

her out the back door since, with all the stir, we can't
do it now. Be careful. If it's quiet, we can take her
out without being seen.

"Now, I've gotta get back into the kitchen to
supervise clean up and laying out of the kitchen ready
for the breakfast staff. Okay, off you go."

"Mom, what are you going to do after we take her
out? Let her go then?"

"Oh, no. You'll see."

"Won't they eventually search these rooms?"

"They can't. I took both keys for this one off the
board and hid them. I won't even have one on me
after I leave here now, and I can make sure they know
the rooms have been locked all the time. The staff
will back that up."

"Okay. Well, you be careful, Mom."

"Get going."

And he did.

Without even glancing at Carrie, the woman
switched off the light and left. The lock went click,
and Carrie sat in total silence and darkness, thinking
about revenge—and redemption.

* * *

Bright lights, humidity, rushing activity, and food
smells greeted Ray, Rose, Henry, and Officer Reba
Brown when they entered the kitchen area. If anyone

there was aware of what was going on elsewhere on that floor, no one showed it.

A bellow from Ray stopped all kitchen action. Briefly, he announced the problem and its danger and asked if anyone had seen Carrie or any unusual activity by anyone there. All shook their heads or said no.

Henry said softly, "Let's talk to each one privately. Get them to line up, women and men separately. Someone has to know something. Rose, you and Officer Reba Brown, take the women. Ray can talk to the men by himself since there are fewer of them. You know what you need to find out. Any unusual activity, break in routine, or, of course, anyone writing on a paper muffin cup."

Ray said, "Officer Brown is assigned to watch the back door to this area."

"That's okay. I'm going to check the rest of the area Rose mentioned, and I can keep an eye on the back door for now."

If anyone noticed Henry was taking control and even bossing what would have been his superior officer, no one mentioned it.

Henry was back quickly and shouted above the dishwasher noise, "Who has the keys to those rooms on the hall, and what's in them?"

A male voice said, "There's an office the head chefs use, and the other two rooms are storage for the banquet area. The back door should be locked. It's never opened, except for deliveries. The room doors are also kept locked, and they were definitely locked after the dining area was set up yesterday."

"I'd like to check them. Where are the keys?" The man stepped forward and pointed to a board fastened near the kitchen's opening into the main hall. There were three unmarked hooks, and all had keys on them. Henry took the keys and returned to the hall. He tried two keys in the first door and, when the third worked, found that, indeed, one room was a small office. It was sparsely furnished—a desk, filing cabinets, three chairs, but otherwise empty. No closet. None of the keys fit the second room. He tried them all again with no luck. The third room opened easily with the first key he tried. It was full of chairs and stacked tablecloths. But the middle room...?

He returned to the kitchen and, after sending Officer Brown to guard the back door, questioned the staff about a missing key. No one admitted to any knowledge as to why the keys to the middle room were gone and remaining keys had been re-distributed to all the hooks.

Reba Brown beckoned to Henry from the kitchen

entrance. When he joined her in the hall, she said, "Sir, when we questioned the workers, one woman admitted the head chef was gone for an unusually long time during the past hour and told them she was checking that all was going smoothly with table cleanup in the dining area. But the server had been working out there and didn't see her. She doesn't want anyone to know she told me that."

"Thank you, Officer. We will respect her privacy. Is the head chef in the kitchen?"

"No, sir. She left a bit ago, saying she wanted to be sure the snack trays on the bar were full, but I suppose she should be back at any minute."

"Okay. When we find my wife, as well as whoever did this, and arrest them, then you can safely tell me who informed you about the chef's absence, but we will still try to keep her name out of it if we need that information for a trial."

Officer Brown nodded and returned to the back door, but Henry remained in the hall. *When! When! When we find my wife. Oh, Carrie, where are you? God keep you safe.*

He followed a large woman in a white jacket back into the kitchen and stopped her to ask if she was the head chef.

"I am. How may I help you?"

"I would like the key to that middle storage room."

"The keys are kept on that board." She pointed.

"The key to the middle room is missing."

"It can't be."

"Do you have personal keys?"

"No, all keys are kept on the board. Now, can my staff go back to work? We need to finish clean up and then set up for the breakfast crew who will be coming to work here in," she looked at a wall clock, "three hours."

Henry motioned to Ray and Rose, and all three left the kitchen area. As soon as they had reached the banquet room, he said, "I think I've met that head chef somewhere. I can't remember where now, but it could very possibly be related to some case I worked. I'll think about it, but, in the meantime, I'd like to send Officer Brown back to monitor activity in the kitchen. Can you get someone else to cover the back door so Brown can find a stool or chair in there and watch all that's going on, including paying concealed, but special, attention to the actions of the head chef? Something seems fishy about her."

"Okay," Ray said. "And I've been thinking that Carrie's abduction stems from something in your past here. Your feeling you have seen the chef before tends to confirm it."

"Yes, I've been afraid of the same thing, and now," he almost whispered the words, "Carrie is suffering because of that."

* * *

God bless Jerry. Carrie easily freed her hands and spent a few moments rubbing her arms to get circulation working. She stretched her arms forward and back. She was sure Jerry had meant for the ties to be loose and was grateful. However, the knots in the tie binding her feet felt like they were much tighter. She needed scissors—or that knife he had held—to cut those. His mother had been watching him as he tied her feet. Perhaps that made the difference.

She felt the knot on the towel strips around her waist and worked on it until it came loose, but her feet remained fastened to the chair.

She had seen the switch and remembered its location, so she began a lift, push, and bang toward the wall that held it.

Her journey toward the light switch seemed to take forever, but eventually she made it and, mustering all her strength, lifted her body and the chair high enough so she could reach the switch.

Ah. She blinked, shut her eyes for a few moments, opened them, and surveyed her prison. No knife in sight. She sat quietly, praying for guidance to her next action.

* * *

After the head chef returned to the kitchen, she spent time making sure all her staff was performing as expected. Then she called out a few names and told those called to begin putting clean tablecloths from storage room three on the dining room tables, following up with napkins and silverware. She pointed to the keyboard hooks. "That cop messed up the keys, but there should be keys there that work on room three."

Reba, watching her as closely as she dared, noticed the chef then went to a drawer at the back of the kitchen area and took out something small. Maybe a key? Reba popped off her stool and followed the assigned workers toward the storage room. Looking in the open door to room three, Reba saw only chairs and neatly stacked tablecloths. So, this was one of the two storage rooms.

She felt sure the chef had taken a key or keys from that drawer, and, returning to the kitchen, she walked boldly to it. It held spatulas in many sizes. She poked at them, seeing nothing else, and headed back to her stool. The chef came up to her and said, "You realize, for health reasons, we are going to have to wash everything in that drawer. Now, keep your hands off our equipment, and stop bothering us."

Glad for an excuse to leave without causing suspicion, Officer Reba Brown walked out of the kitchen, thinking she needed to find Major King or Deputy Chief Duncan. When she got to the dining room, she saw both men and hurried to them. "I think I know where the keys to that middle room were hidden and that the chef now has them on her person. If you'll come back to the kitchen..."

* * *

When the door to her prison room began opening, Carrie was again filled with hope, then instantly lost that when the chef reappeared.

"How did you get the light on?" she asked. "Oh, never mind, I see your hands are free. Trust Jerry to make a mess of things. Now, where did he put the knife?"

"I think he took it with him," Carrie said, "and he told me about Mikey, why he was in prison, and how he died. I am so, so sorry. I have a son near Mikey's age, so I think I can understand, in a small way, your grief and a tiny bit of what you have had to suffer."

Carrie was speaking words she hadn't had time to think about. They were just coming, and it looked like the woman was paying attention, so she continued.

"You can be proud of Jerry. He understands very well how you feel about Mikey, and also how I now feel about something I knew nothing of until tonight. Jerry is a kind and caring man, and he needs to be kept out of any trouble with the law. Don't you want to help him do that? You've certainly had more than enough dealings with the legal system than anyone would want to handle. But you had two sons, and the one you still have is certainly worth helping. As you can see, he did the best he could to give me a chance to free myself but didn't want to go against your wishes, so didn't do it openly. Now, we both need to do all we can to save Jerry. I believe we have it in our power to keep him out of any police activity that may be coming."

The woman stood still, staring at her. Carrie almost stopped breathing, not wanting to interrupt what was undoubtedly a make-or-break moment. Then, to Carrie's astonishment, tears began running down the chef's face. Carrie watched and then bowed her head.

Silence continued until Carrie heard a loud snuffle and looked up to see the woman had grabbed a dish towel and was blowing her nose. Again, she looked at Carrie and finally said, "You seem like a nice person. I didn't think about you being a nice person. I just wanted revenge for Mikey, and you're married to the man who put him in prison."

"Henry and I have been married only about a year, so I didn't know him here in Kansas City, but I do know how much some of the things he had to do for his job here give him grief. Did you hear about the award he got tonight?"

"A bit. Something about saving lives. But, why not my Mikey's life?"

"Believe me, he is going to grieve for Mikey when he learns what happened. He believes in truth and justice, but, in this case, it seems the law failed to put that to work for Mikey. I have heard the story from Jerry, and, honestly, I wish I could protect Police Major Henry King from hearing it. His grief over what happened to Mikey is going to give you plenty of revenge. But it will be my job to comfort him through this nightmare. I love him deeply and know what a good man he really is. But I want to help lift your grief as well. I think one big step will be found in fully honoring the son you still have.

"Now then, we need to plan how we are going to face the police officers who will come here. Please untie my feet. Then we'll think about justice for you and for Mikey, as well as for the police officers who are probably missing some of the evening's celebration because they're searching for me. We can't erase all you have brought about this night, but we can lighten your load."

Carrie kept talking while the chef got down on her knees to untie her feet. "There are people out there who are undoubtedly quite upset, especially my husband. Since we don't want to bring Jerry into this, I will say I have learned what happened to Mikey and imply it came from you. If you feel ready to talk about it, you can tell them Mikey's story from the beginning at the convenience store, but first, I need to tell you all that Jerry told me. You may not know everything he learned from his brother.

"First, can you call Jerry and ask him to stay home, and will he listen?"

The woman was already poking on her phone. "It's Mom. Things have taken a new turn and the lady is free. Yes, she is a good person. Now, you stay home, and do not come back to get involved in more of this. No, no, no, I'm fine, I'm fine.

"I mean it. Stay home. Officer King's wife and I are working things out."

The chef put her phone away as Carrie said, "My name is Carrie. What's yours?"

"Glenna. Glenna McDougal."

"Okay, Glenna. You are going to have to admit your initial actions. I did, after all, disappear. How do you feel about that?"

Glenna McDougal pulled up a chair, sat, and looked at her lap. "I guess embarrassment and maybe shame. My thoughts about revenge for Mikey went out of me like air out of a balloon when you talked about Jerry. Can't change the past, but Jerry is a good son, and I haven't done enough to let him know I think that. I was so involved with Mikey's problems, I kinda forgot Jerry. I still hurt inside about Mikey, but now I realize I am mother to another son who is very important to me." There were more tears and more use of the towel as a hanky before Glenna said, "And, I do love him, Carrie. I love him, as I know you love your son. What's your son's name?"

"Rob—for Robert."

"Rob, for Robert," Glenna repeated as she reached out to take Carrie's hand.

"I can promise you," Carrie said, "that when you see my husband's reaction after he learns about Mikey's death, any revenge you felt you needed will be taken care of and healed."

"I like that word 'healed,'" Glenna McDougal said as the door opened, Officer Reba Brown looked in at them, gasped, took out her gun, and hurried toward Glenna.

"No, no," Carrie said. "We're fine, Glenna is no threat. No need to bother her."

"Are you...are you all right?" Officer Brown asked. "Shouldn't I take charge of this woman?"

"No need. The chef and I have come to an understanding, and she's not going anywhere."

"Miss," the chef said, "could you please ask a server in the kitchen to bring us something to drink? Would you like a cup of tea, Carrie?"

"No, but water would be good, and, Officer, would you please find my husband and Chief Duncan?"

Reba Brown stared at them for a minute, then disappeared.

In a few minutes, a server came in with two water goblets on a tray. That was followed shortly by a hubbub equivalent to, Carrie thought, what might accompany a stampeding herd of elephants, and Henry and Ray stood in the doorway, followed by a babbling crowd of banquet attendees.

Carrie was soon wrapped in a Henry hug, and Ray had begun talking with Chef Glenna McDougal. A rotating mass of police officers, none of whom were now showing weapons, crowded in and around the doorway, and, when they observed the scene in the room, fell silent as they moved away so others could see in.

As soon as she could speak, Carrie said, "You guys pull up chairs. Glenna and I have quite a story to tell."

THE TWINS FOLLOW A TRAIL

"Yuck." Jeremy whispered.

He looked over at his sister's plate and repeated, "Yuck."

Jemima pointed to the cauliflower hill on one side of her plate. "Yes, but you can build with it."

Patricia and Randy had been busy talking about grown-up stuff, but now turned toward the twins. Jemima's hand moved quickly to hide the cauliflower hill, but Momma didn't look at her plate. Instead she said, "Nana Eleanor and Popi Jason have invited us to fly to Arkansas for Thanksgiving."

"Yea," said Jemima, forgetting about her cauliflower hill as Jeremy bounced in his chair and echoed, "Yea."

"And," Momma said, smiling, "we'll have Thanksgiving dinner at the Ozark Folk Center State Park where you went with Nana and Popi last summer. Aunt Carrie and Uncle Henry are coming too. Daddy and I want to see the park, and I'll do some Christmas shopping in the Crafts Village while we're there."

"TOYS," the twins shouted.

"Seems to me Nana and Popi pretty well loaded you up with toys from there last summer," Daddy said. "Wooden cars, corn shuck dolls, a patchwork bear, handmade puzzles, and games. What more can there be?"

"Patches needs a friend," Jemima said.

"More cars," Jeremy said. "If we get more cars, we can play racetrack."

"We'll go see Maggie and ride the donkey-go-round," Jemima said.

"Donkey-go-round, donkey-go-round," the twins began chanting, "yea, yea, YEA."

Momma and Daddy seemed not to notice that the twins' shouts were quite a bit louder than usually allowed at family meals.

* * *

Thanksgiving dinner was over.

"Oof," said Aunt Carrie.

"Oof indeed," echoed Popi Jason as he held the restaurant door open for everyone.

"What's oof?" asked Jemima.

"Means we ate a lot," Uncle Henry said, "and we feel stuffed. Here, kids, let's hold hands while we cross the street to the Crafts Village."

"S'posed to clean your plates, so oof is good," Jemima said, with all the wisdom of a five-year-old.

As soon as they were inside the Crafts Village, Jemima began hopping from one foot to the other. "Donkey-go-round, donkey-go-round," she chanted. "Let's go see Maggie."

Jeremy joined the chant and the hopping.

"What are they talking about?" Momma asked. "They mentioned a donkey as soon as I told them we were coming here for Thanksgiving."

"The donkey pushes a ride that's sort of like a merry-go-round," said Nana. "They rode it a jillion times last summer. Swinging benches are fastened to a huge circular wheel with a canvas umbrella over it. The wheel turns on a spindle in the center, but there's no motor. A donkey provides the power by pushing a bar fastened to the spindle. The JJs liked the donkey as much as the ride. They spent so much time there they got to help feed her."

Nana looked down at the twins. "The carousel is way at the other end of the Crafts Village. Your mother, Aunt Carrie, and I want to do some Christmas shopping before we go there. Last summer you liked visiting the craft shops. Remember watching the man who makes tops on a foot-powered lathe and the lady who weaves baskets?"

Jemima stared at the ground, digging the toe of her shoe into a patch of dry grass. "Uhn-huh."

Daddy said, "While you girls shop, I'd like to visit the blacksmith's forge Jason told me about. You guys want to come along?"

"Sure thing," Uncle Henry said. "He helped me make a trivet when Carrie and I were here last month."

Popi looked down at his grandson. "Jeremy, why don't you come with us? You and I can also visit the man who makes wooden toys."

Jeremy glanced at his sister and saw her nod her head toward the south-east corner of the Craft Village, so he nodded too.

"Okay, then," Nana said. "We'll split up. Patricia, Carrie, Jemima, and I will Christmas shop. Let's meet at the outdoor stage in two hours. Musicians are performing there all day, so no one will mind waiting if one group is a little late."

For a while Jeremy followed the men while Jemima lagged farther and farther behind Momma, Nana, and Aunt Carrie. When the women went into the Country Kitchen Shop, Jemima stayed outside, pretending to watch several children playing hide and seek around the craft huts. Then, as if taking part in the game, she ran around a hut.

A few minutes later, Momma Patricia asked her mother, "Where's Jemima?"

"I'm sure she went after Jeremy. You know how hard it is to separate those two. This whole area is enclosed inside a high wooden fence and exits are only through the administration building or gift shop, so there's no worry. During their visits last summer, they made a lot of friends here. I bet most of the workers already recognize them, and they both know the Craft Village quite well. I'm sure Jemima wanted to visit the forge. She went there with Jeremy several times last summer. In fact, they watched the blacksmith make letter openers—from a safe distance, of course—though the smith did allow them to touch the iron he was going to work with before he heated it. I didn't want to tell you when the men were with us, but, with money I gave them, they bought two letter openers they insisted they helped make to give to their dad and grandfather for Christmas."

Momma Patricia laughed. "What a special place this is."

At about the same time, Jason asked his son-in-law, "Randy, where's Jeremy?"

"Went with Jemima and the girls. Hard to separate those two."

* * *

Meanwhile each twin had circled craft huts and slipped through crowds, passing the pottery studio, weaving hut, quilting shop, and the Old Time Print Shop. They both arrived near the donkey carousel at about the same moment and stopped, staring at the vacant area.

At last Jeremy said, "Nobody here."

Jemima nodded. "No donkey man, nobody coming to ride. Where's Maggie?"

"Let's go see," Jeremy said, tugging his sister around the carousel toward the small pasture where the donkey stayed between rides.

They stood together, looking through the pasture's pipe gate. The grassy yard was empty.

"Empty," Jemima said. "Wonder where Maggie is."

Jeremy pointed, "Food bucket empty. Just poop there."

"Donkey poop?"

"'Course, silly."

"Not silly." She shoved at him, and they both giggled.

Just then the donkey man came into the yard through the back gate, followed by a park ranger. Both were frowning.

Jemima tugged at Jeremy and tried to hide, but Jeremy, ignoring the tug, asked, voice wavering a bit at first, "W-where...where's Maggie?"

"Hello kids." The man looked at them for a minute, still frowning. Then he smiled and said, "Say, I remember you two from last summer. You had a lot of fun with Maggie. I'm sorry, but someone took your friend away when they weren't supposed to. We're looking for her now."

Neither Jeremy nor Jemima could think of anything to say but, "Oh." Then they turned away and moved along the board fence surrounding the area.

Suddenly Jemima said, "Poop," and pulled on Jeremy's jacket sleeve. "See there, more donkey poop over by the big gate."

When they got to the plank gate, they looked back at the donkey pasture. The men were gone. Then they stared down at the tell-tale poop. A padlock with shiny scratches all over it lay on the ground next to the poop, and the chain that usually laced through a hole in each gate hung in only one hole.

Jeremy said, "Lock fell off. Let's open the gate. Maggie prob'ly went outside."

"Maybe we should go get Momma and Daddy," Jemima said.

"They're shopping. They won't want to come. We'll go find them after we find Maggie. Everyone will say we did good. C'mon, help me push the gate."

Working together, they shoved the gate open. As soon as they were through, it swung shut with a *chunk*.

"It's just a parking lot," Jemima said. "Why would Maggie want to see a dumb old parking lot?"

"Look," Jeremy pointed. "Over there, an open place in the fence. Maybe Maggie went there."

They started running across the asphalt, not seeing a Folk Center Trolley as it began an end turn by the gate. The trolley honked, stopped, and the driver came to the door. "Hey kids, you shouldn't be out here by yourselves. It's not safe. Where's your family?" Mutely, Jeremy pointed at the opening in the fence and pulled Jemima toward it, running around the front of the trolley. When they got to the opening in the fence they looked back. The driver waved, shut the trolley door, and continued on his way.

* * *

Meanwhile, Nana, Momma, and Carrie had reached the music shed first, and when the men came, Popi said, "Sorry, we got interested in the woodcarver's stories and, well, that guy is something else, he told us..."

Patricia's panicky voice stopped him. "Where are the twins?"

After everyone babbled explanations about why they thought both twins were with the other group, Popi Jason said, "I bet they've gone to the donkey carousel. I'll go get them. Don't worry, the grounds are fenced and most workers here know them."

* * *

As soon as the bus drove off, the JJs stopped running and looked at the opening they'd found. It was shielded by a short piece of fencing built out into the parking lot. Jemima stared at the sign above the opening and sounded out the letters. "R-V. Puh-rr...oh, park!"

"RV Park," Jeremy shouted. "More park. Let's go."

They walked into a wide corridor leading to the second park.

Jemima stopped and lifted her foot. "Look," she said, "donkey poop. Stinks."

"Maggie's here," Jeremy said.

When they were through the opening, they saw huge trailers parked everywhere.

"Travel houses. Daddy calls them RVs."

They hurried along a row of trailers, finding a friendly dog tied to a tree, but no donkey.

A voice shouted, "Hey, kids, you lost?"

A large man with a beard shut the door to his trailer and began walking toward them.

"No. We're looking for Maggie," Jemima said.

"She your dog?"

"No, a donkey."

He snorted. "No donkey here. You two go on back to your folks. You know the way?"

Jeremy pushed his sister behind him. "We know. We're going." He and Jemima turned and ran toward the next row of trailers.

"He looked mean," Jemima said.

"I don't see Maggie," Jeremy said, "but she's gotta be here somewhere since she pooped in the entrance. There's a street over there. Let's go follow it."

Jemima pulled at his jacket. "We aren't supposed to go in a street without Momma or Daddy, or the lady with the stop sign at school."

"We can't go back where that man is, and everyone would want us to find Maggie. Don't be a sissy."

"Not a sissy."

Jeremy stopped walking. "Don't you want to find Maggie?" he asked.

"Yes, but Momma and Daddy can help."

For a moment he hesitated, then, making his

voice very big, said, "I'm gonna find Maggie first, whether you're here or not. Finding her is a good thing, okay? You can go back if you want."

Both of them stood still, looking at their shoes. Finally, Jemima, afraid to go back by herself, murmured a tiny, "Okay," and trudged after her brother.

* * *

The twins couldn't hear the park-wide announcement being broadcast over the public address system. "Two children are missing somewhere in the Craft Village. They're twins, five years old, a boy and a girl with blond hair. They're dressed in jeans, yellow sweatshirts, and blue jackets. If you find them, call 555-6900 or bring them to the administration building. Jeremy and Jemima, if you hear this, please go to the nearest craft hut and ask the person there to bring you to the administration building."

Jeremy and Jemima also didn't know that Momma was sitting in a chair in the administration building trying not to cry, while Nana patted her arm and murmured, "We know they've got to be somewhere inside the fenced grounds. They just wandered away from the carousel area when they saw no one was there. We also know God is watching over them, wherever they are."

Daddy, Popi, Uncle Henry, and two park rangers

were on the other side of the room talking about a search plan. Aunt Carrie stood in a corner with her eyes shut, just like the twins knew how to do for prayers in Sunday School.

Suddenly Carrie raised her head and said, "I'm going to the carousel while the rest of you search. They might come back there."

"Good idea," one ranger said. "The rest of us will spread out and work our way through the craft area from the administration building to the auditorium and gift shop."

* * *

"Lots of cars," Jemima said, backing away from the street.

Jeremy hesitated only a moment. "I'm not scared. We're in the grass next to the street. Cars don't drive on grass. Let's look for more poop."

The two of them walked slowly along the road-side, eyes on the ground.

Then Jeremy lifted his head and said, "Look over there, Jemmy."

* * *

For a while Carrie sat quietly in one of the carousel swings with her eyes shut. Then she decided to walk around the area. Maybe the twins had left some sign.

A man came into the pasture carrying a bucket, and Carrie hurried over to the pipe gate. "Have you seen five-year-old twins around here this afternoon?" she asked.

He nodded. "Sure did. They came to see the donkey, and I had to tell them Maggie had been stolen. They left after that."

"Stolen!"

"Yes. I brought her in before daylight to get ready before the day's rides, then went for my coffee. When I came back, this gate was open, the chain was off the gate over there, and she was gone. Thing is, I don't usually shut the padlock on that gate chain since you can't reach it from the other side anyway, so it must have been an inside job." He shook his head sadly. "One of us."

"Oh, my goodness, the kids are missing too. Didn't you hear the announcements?"

"No. I've been outside the park talking to the police. Surely those two will be somewhere in the craft area. I'll go see if I can help search." He put down his bucket and hurried away while Carrie continued her walk around the carousel yard.

When she came to the wooden gate, she stopped, seeing that the gate's chain hung from one side only. Then she looked at the ground. There was a padlock

lying next to a pile of what must be donkey drop-
pings. She didn't touch the lock, but bent to study
it, seeing that it was covered with irregular shiny
scratch marks. *I wonder,* she thought, *could those be
a donkey's teeth marks?* She pushed the gate open.

It didn't take her long to find the squished poop
and the opening into the RV Park. "Did you see a
donkey, or two five-year-olds in here?" she asked a
woman who was walking briskly down a road lined
with motor homes.

The woman stopped, looking startled. "A donkey?
Children? No, I didn't see them. I just started my
daily walk, though. They could have been here
earlier."

A man called from his seat in the sun outside a
nearby trailer. "They were here just a bit ago. Said
they were looking for a donkey. Didn't believe a
word of it. Told 'em to get on back to their folks.
They said they would and went that way." He stood
and pointed. "I s'posed they belonged to somebody
staying here in the park."

Carrie thanked him, took out her cell phone, and
dialed the administration building. "I'm hot on the
trail of the twins," she said. "I think they left the craft
grounds through the parking lot gate near the donkey
yard. I've traced them into the RV Park next door

where a man saw them not long ago. I'm beginning a search here now."

She listened, then said, "Yes, do come help me look. See you in a few minutes."

She stuck the phone in her pocket and headed in the direction the man had pointed.

When Carrie reached the street, she looked both ways, wondering where to go next. "Jeremy! Jemima!" No reply.

The kids might have thought someone took the donkey along the street, but in which direction?

Then she saw several people crossing the street about half a block away. As Carrie got closer, she decided they were coming to look at a nativity scene set up in a yard across from the RV Park.

When she was close enough to see inside the shed sheltering life-sized figures of Mary, Joseph, and the baby Jesus, she began laughing. Two small children were trying to remove a very real donkey from the nativity scene. The reluctant donkey was about to finish eating all the hay that had been scattered on the ground.

"C'mon Maggie," said one child, shoving against the donkey's side.

"Gotta go home right now, and I <u>mean</u> it!" said the other child, tugging on the donkey's halter.

The placid donkey ignored them and lifted her head to the manger, still temptingly full of sweet hay. The plastic baby went *clunk* against the manger's edge as Carrie hurried forward and said, "Hi," to Jeremy and Jemima.

"We found Maggie, Aunt Carrie. She was lost, and we found her all by ourselves." They were both grinning and didn't seem even a tiny bit surprised to see her.

The growing audience outside the shed applauded when Carrie lifted the baby Jesus away from donkey teeth and cradled him in her left arm as she took out her cell phone.

PLANNING A CRIME—AND A WEDDING

Shirley pushed the cookie plate closer and said, "You ready to plan a wedding, now that your son and Catherine cheated us out of a wedding by marrying on their own in Oklahoma?"

Carrie, busy chewing one of her friend's special prune-pecan cookies, widened her eyes and managed only a questioning, mouth-closed, "Huummm?"

"Seems there's been somethin' more than just friendship going on since Dana Jean came into our life and Junior met her."

Carrie swallowed and said, "So, you think maybe..."

"Yes, maybe. Given Junior's history with women, not sure I dare hope. He's had three or four lady friends in the past few years but nothing came of any of those, and I gave up thinking about a wedding a long time ago. Seems those women were all just what I said, lady friends, and nothing moved as far as wedding talk."

"Oh, Shirley, it would be thrilling if those two

did get married. I know we all like Dana Jean and her brother a lot. But, well, why do you think this friendship might become more than just another friendship for Junior?"

"You ever figure something was going on in your son's life before he talked about it?"

After a silence, Carrie said, "I see what you mean."

"It's a momma thing, and for now, we keep quiet about what I think. But, can't stop my thinkin'." Shirley sighed, then laughed. "Maybe I'll get a grandbaby here yet. Possible. Junior just turned 35, and I think Dana Jean is only a bit beyond 30.

"So now, don't forget you and me are taking the two of them to visit history museums in town in a couple of days when Dana has a day off and Donnie is with Roger and our helper and the cows. But don't you dare give a peep or a wink about what I'm thinkin'."

Shirley picked up a cookie, took a bite, chewed, and then tilted her head, looking thoughtful. "Carrie, tell me honest how you like the cookies. I was out of raisins, so I chopped up some prunes I had on the shelf."

"They're good. Prunes are a bit squishier than the raisins, but they taste just as good. Let me take a couple to Henry now. I'll report on what he says."

"Okay, but no hint about what I hope for with the kids."

Shirley paused, then twinkled at Carrie. "Oh, never mind. I'm betting you'll tell Henry, but I already know he's okay at keeping secrets if you ask him to."

And, of course, that afternoon, Henry promised to do just that.

* * *

Since it was a weekday morning, Shirley easily found a parking space in front of the newly opened expansion to the Rogers Historical Museum. No one had done much talking on the ride into town, and Carrie wondered if Junior and Dana were holding hands in the back seat. Once upon a time that would have signified more than a casual interest and, these days, maybe it still did—even more than a passion-filled kiss. Ah! She had learned after her marriage to Henry that, under the right circumstances, passion was relatively easy, even for mature couples. In her opinion, however, gentle hand holding signified something deeper between two adults.

Junior held the museum entry door open for the women, and they were greeted by an attendant, who suggested they begin their self-guided tour on the right. Almost immediately the four of them separated as they walked and looked. Dana, newly back to the Northwest Arkansas Ozarks after leaving the area in her teens, spent the most time studying each photograph and glass-enclosed display. It was, Carrie thought, as if she wanted to memorize history she had missed while she was gone. Her interest in events that had happened during her lifetime, as well as the years prior to her birth, reminded Carrie that her father's tight and crushing control had probably kept her from many normal activities, and even museum visits, during her childhood and early teens.

Carrie stayed behind Dana, curious about what she would find most interesting here. Eventually Dana's progress stalled before one of the photographs. Carrie stopped and spent at least a minute staring at the picture of a long-ago mayor and his dog who was, the legend said, named Majority and called Major for short.

After what she considered a reasonable time, Carrie moved to stand beside Dana. "Find something especially interesting?" she asked, then continued, "Oh, the 1980 payroll robbery at the City Canning Company. Henry's always been interested in that because the robbers were never found, and neither was any of the money. One of the robbers shot two employees who, thank goodness, recovered. Sounds like something out of today's news, doesn't it? An unusually large amount of money was involved. The company was really humming back then. They had a lot of temporary employees to be paid in cash, since the harvesting of apples and other crops was in full swing."

"Uh-huh," Dana said as she turned away to walk down the wall of pictures while Carrie studied the photo taken during what must have been a close aftermath of the robbery, since it showed an ambulance with a crowd of people clustered around it.

"My goodness, this is interesting," Carrie said, wondering why Dana had suddenly lost interest in the photograph and accompanying newspaper clipping. "The newspaper headline calls the two men 'The kitchen bandits.' It says they both wore printed flour sacks, with eye holes cut in them, over their heads and had on shirts that looked like they had been made from a red-and-white-checked tablecloth.

"I guess it took the police a long time to get there because the men and the money had disappeared by the time officers arrived, and the thieves weren't found during an area search. I wonder why there weren't guards with the payroll."

"Those two men who were shot were guards," Dana said, then turned her head away, and finished,

"Well, I suppose they were, at least."

Carrie read the newspaper clipping with the photo more carefully and realized it said nowhere that the two wounded men had been guards. Ah well, probably thinking they were guards was a natural assumption.

Now her mind was whirring. *Wouldn't the guards have been armed? Did the robbers know the routine for payroll delivery so well they had intended from the beginning to shoot, maybe even kill, the two guards to get them out of the way? The robbers were obviously able to come on the two men so suddenly there was no time for defensive action. Henry had said more than once that the robbery took a huge amount of prior knowledge and planning.*

Carrie looked back at Dana, who had moved farther down the row of photographs and was now studying the picture of an early day family reunion. Junior came in the room and, realizing her presence probably would put a damper on any show of affection she was hoping to see, Carrie went to the next display area and joined Shirley in a study of farming equipment and hand tools.

An hour later the four of them returned to the car and headed for Shiloh Museum of Ozark History in Springdale.

This museum was one of Carrie's favorites. Displays were arranged almost like a maze, and there were surprises around every corner, including one wall where you suddenly came on the front of an enormous and very shiny, new eighteen-wheeler truck cab with lots of bright red paint and chrome. It looked like a giant had sawed off the front of a real Peterbilt truck and glued it to the museum wall. As it was, the truck seemed to be barreling down on the viewer, and the first time she turned a corner and saw it, Carrie jumped in a "get out of the way" reflex. But she had soon fallen in love with that truck and sometimes touched it on a headlight when she walked by. It was there, she knew, in honor of trucking companies that had been active in North-west Arkansas for many years.

As had happened in the Rogers Museum, the four of them separated. Though wanting to watch and see how Dana and Junior reacted to their first view of the big truck, Carrie responded to a tickling memory that had begun stirring in her thoughts when she viewed the photograph and information about the 1980 canning company robbery in Rogers. She moved immediately to a bench in front of Shiloh museum's rotating photo display of people and events in Northwest Arkansas from the 1950s through the 1980s. The rotation was continuous, so what she was looking for eventually appeared. Ah, she was right, there it was, and the photo had a date. July 1979. The photo rotation continued, and she still sat on the bench, thinking. By the time the 1979 photo of several men loading crates of apples in a farm truck rotated around again, she had decided and went to look for Dana.

* * *

This time she found Junior and Dana together, talking about what they were seeing and pointing at various display objects. Junior was saying, "Wish I had a mouse and could get into that chicken feeder display. Mouse would go for the chicken feed, wouldn't he!" Dana's response was a happy, light-hearted sounding giggle.

Carrie hesitated, then turned away. Let her find the photograph on her own. That meant Carrie wanted to stay close to the rotating photos, so she moved to the other side of the viewing area, the one where photos were dated 1990s to 2010s and settled on the bench there to wait.

"You sure are stuck on those pictures," Shirley said as she came to sit next to Carrie. "It's like you had family members here, though I know full well you didn't."

"I just enjoy seeing them," Carrie said. "Where are Dana and Junior?"

"I dunno. There's a lot to see in here, and you can almost get lost looking at it. Once upon a time I was in here and got caught short. At first I couldn't find the right way out, and I almost didn't make it to the Ladies' in time. Whenever I'm at this museum I test myself in here to see if I can remember where to find a display I want to see again.

"Oh, there the kids are!" She raised her voice. "Do you two want to come sit on that bench and see some old timey pictures? Old timey to you, that is. Carrie and I both think they're interesting, though Carrie has no connection to any of the people or goings-on they show."

With only smiles and nods, Dana and Junior came to sit on the bench across from Carrie and Shirley. When Shirley started to tell Carrie how she'd made clothing on an old treadle sewing machine like one shown in a photo, Carrie held a finger to her lips and pointed across the two viewing screens toward Junior and Dana.

In a short time Dana said, "Oh! That man! That's my father, and he has on a red-and-white-checked shirt like...Oh...where did they get that picture?"

Shirley looked at Carrie and, speaking very softly,

said, "You know about the kitchen bandits and the canning company robbery?" A nod from Carrie was her only answer.

Dana stood, twisted back and forth as if trying to decide which way to turn, and finally stepped away from the bench. Instead of moving on to see another display, she shut her eyes and stood, statue still, in the middle of the floor. Junior looked over at his mother and Carrie, put his hands up in a "what's going on" gesture, then went to put an arm around Dana. "What is it? What's wrong, Dana?"

Carrie, thankful that there were no other museum visitors in the room at that time, said, "I think we need to talk. Maybe it would be best if we all sat here by the photo displays."

When Junior had led a numb-looking Dana back to the viewing bench, Carrie told him, "Dana's reacting to the red-and-white-checked shirt her father is wearing in a picture you saw over there. That picture was taken in 1979 when several men were loading crates of apples in the back of a truck. And, in the Rogers Museum, Dana and I both saw a photo showing the aftermath of a payroll robbery at the City Canning Company in 1980. The two payroll guards were shot, and the robbers got away very quickly. At the time, a newspaper headline called the robbers the kitchen bandits, since the men were wearing shirts made of a checked fabric like that often used for kitchen tablecloths, and both also had printed cloth flour sacks with cut-out eye holes pulled over their heads. Henry and I come to programs at this museum quite often, and I usually take time to look at the pictures you see over there. I remembered that tablecloth shirt though, of course, I didn't know it was Floyd Jackson wearing it. But the shirt mentioned is unusual enough that I wondered today if there was some kind of connection to the payroll robbery. Dana, you did show a special interest in the photo we saw in Rogers and seemed to know something about it, so I waited for you to see the picture here, wondering if you could identify it more fully. The conclusion I suspect we both have come to is that your father may have had something to do with that robbery. Fortunately, as we read at the museum in Rogers, though two men who were probably guards were shot, both recovered. Neither the robbers nor the payroll money was ever found.

"Dana, you think the shirt mentioned in the Rogers newspaper article was your dad's, don't you?"

At first, Carrie thought maybe Dana wasn't going to answer. Instead, she looked down and pushed at the cuticle on one of her nails, but she finally looked up and said, "Probably. I remember seeing scraps of material with red and white checks in a bag of cleaning rags at our house when I was a little girl. I guess it could have been from a shirt—or shirts. Momma said the scraps were from a stained table-cloth one of the ladies she housecleaned for had given her. I asked if I could have the scraps to make a doll dress, and she said no. That rag bag is still in the back of a closet at the house, left there after all these years, and I have seen something red in it. The bag was probably left because no one was interested in what looked like trash when they took away all the furniture and household things. I remember thinking the red fabric in the bag was probably part of a shirt, but I haven't taken time to dig down for it yet."

"I'm sorry," Carrie said. "I guess I should have warned you about the shirt I had seen in a picture here. I was pretty sure it was the same design the Rogers article mentioned."

Dana pulled away from the arm Junior had put around her. "I reckon we lived on that stolen money for a long time. Since Daddy was no good at farming, or at staying long with any other job, I have wondered where much of our live-on money came from. I knew Momma couldn't make all of it cleaning houses, though she was sometimes hired part time to do extra work at the canning company office. I guess that was because she was always good at math. Thank goodness she wasn't there during the robbery."

After a pause, Dana said, "Of course the money is long gone, and there is no way I can ever earn enough to pay it back."

"Canning company's been closed for years," Shirley said. "I'm sure the money is a dead issue now."

Dana stood and headed out to exhibits across the hallway. When Junior started to follow, Shirley put up a restraining hand and said, "Not now, Son. Give her a bit of time to think and adjust."

* * *

The drive home was even quieter than the one to town had been, and Carrie noticed Dana sat at a distance from Junior and looked out the car window on her side all the way home.

When Shirley had parked in front of her house, Junior was out of the car first and hurried around to open the door for Dana. When Carrie slid out and turned toward them, she noticed Dana had been crying and that she stepped away from the arm Junior extended toward her.

"Hold it," Junior said. "You can't get rid of me like that. Maybe news about the robbery seems a big thing to you, but it isn't to me, so that's that. It makes no difference to me."

Dana said, "Huh. Be careful. I'm the daughter of a thief and murderer, and I'm tainted by that. I'm glad Donnie doesn't know and never needs to know.

"But I wish I knew more about the robbery. Who was the other thief, and did Momma make his shirt as well as Dad's? Is he still alive? Did he and Dad split the money or…or…what? Maybe Dad even killed him and took all the money."

Shirley said, "Oh Dana, no need to think such things. It's all over and done with now."

"It's not over for me," Dana said. "I need to know more. I already knew my father was a bad person, but this? Isn't it possible he was guilty of two murders—killing both my mother and the second thief, as well as the shooting of those guards? What he did reflects on Donnie and on me. I can't just push it all aside and forget it. The sins of the fathers and all that."

"Twaddle," Shirley said, "but tell you what, we'll talk to Lawyer Blevins about it."

* * *

Every one of them wanted to hear Chester Blevins's assessment of the situation, and there were several relieved comments when he said, "Since Miss

Jackson was under eighteen at the time all this happened, left the area soon after, and the suspect she is related to is dead, I don't see how you have to worry about any repercussions from this crime. I do wish, however, that we knew who the second man was. It would, at the least, be interesting and perhaps, even now, he could be charged with armed robbery."

Henry said, "I figure it must have been someone from inside the plant, since how, otherwise, could the men have known so much about the timing of the payroll delivery?"

"I bet we could find out, assuming that person is alive and still in this area," Carrie said.

"Well, how would we do that?" Junior asked.

"By putting a piece in the paper about finding the shirt connected to the robbery in a bag at the old Jackson place. We can give the impression that the money might be found there too."

"But that could cause unfriendly or even dangerous feelings toward Dana and Donnie," Henry said. "Some might think they knew about the money and maybe came back to dig it up—and so on. I have another idea. I bet we can find records with the names of office employees at the cannery back then. We could check to see who's still alive and work from there."

"How about this?" Carrie said. "Let's see what's in the rag bag. If Dana has that shirt, I still say we could give a picture to the local paper with information under the picture saying something about it being related to the canning company robbery. That wouldn't necessarily connect the money to Dana and Donnie's home, but the second man might think Floyd Jackson hid it or even put it in a safe deposit box to wait until things died down. Then he was arrested for murdering his wife and kept in jail. He couldn't get at the money, couldn't spend it, or get it and himself out of the country. Therefore, the second thief might decide to do some investigating."

"Hmmm, okay," Blevins said, as he began to construct a square stack of pencils, log home-fashion, on his desk blotter.

Dana had remained silent throughout the conversation and now said, "Donnie won't understand any of this, and he might even be frightened, depending on how much he overhears. I don't want..." then she stopped and was silent again.

After looking over at her, Junior spoke up, "Putting anything in the paper is not okay. Like Henry said, that could still put Dana and her brother in some danger."

"I don't see that it would," Roger said, "but those

two can sleep at our house, and Junior and I can stay at the Jackson place."

"That's no better," Shirley said. "It's still inviting trouble, just for different people."

"That second person is probably dead anyway," Dana said, "and I don't like that this is getting scary."

"Let's think on it overnight," Henry said, "and look at the contents of that rag bag tomorrow morning before Dana goes to work."

* * *

When Carrie answered the ringing phone at 7:30 the following morning, Shirley said, "Going to see the red shirt at Dana's is off. She called and says it isn't there."

"Oh? Yesterday it sounded to me like she had at least seen something red in that bag recently. But I also remember she said this was getting scary. I don't really blame her for thinking that or for wanting to drop everything."

"I dunno," Shirley said. "I kinda think something odd is up, but there's nothing we can do about that now, so it's off."

Which meant Carrie spent a lot more time than she wanted thinking muddled thoughts about that red-checked shirt.

Henry was just as perplexed as she was. He did

offer what eventually sounded like a logical conclusion to Carrie, as well as to Roger and Shirley. "I
agree that the shirt was possibly still there when we
talked about it in the lawyer's office. I guess Dana
decided Junior was right, and it was time to drop the
whole matter. But I think all of us, and especially
Dana, had worked up to being curious about that
second thief. If that's true, her turning off any further
investigation may simply be because she thought our
solutions to finding the second man sounded scary."

And that was that. Except, as Shirley confided to
Carrie a week later, "This whole dang shirt thing has
somehow shut down the friendship between Dana
and Junior. He calls her, and she cuts him off. He
went to see her at work, and she treated him like a
customer she'd never seen before. Yesterday he
suggested a drive to Buffalo National River on her
day off 'cause she'd said a while back that she'd like
to go there. But she said, 'No, thanks.' He doesn't
talk about his feelings to us, but I can tell he's mighty
unhappy." Shirley sighed. "Well, we'll see."

Donnie, however, continued enjoying his accep-
tance by Roger and Shirley. Dana often left him off
at the farm when she went to work, and he was
learning the names of all the cows.

"He's good at calming the girls down if any of

them get fussy when they're in the milking parlor," Roger said, "and he's learned how to put their feed out in the bins. Actually, he's good help, no matter what others may think about his abilities."

A few days later, Donnie walked up to the house after Dana had let him off by the barn. He had a sack in his hand, and what it held caused Shirley to call Henry and Carrie and invite them down to the house for a piece of her blueberry pie.

When the four of them were seated at the kitchen table, Shirley left for a moment and returned with a red-and-white-checked shirt. It looked odd and, before Shirley said anything, Donnie spoke up. "Dana has a big box with Momma's things in it in her room. It sits on her floor, and it has a lock. When she takes off the lock and looks in the box, she pushes her door shut."

He snickered. "Sometimes the door doesn't shut all the way, and I can see her looking in the box. She was looking in the box yesterday when she got a phone call from where she works about hurrying there. She went off in the car, and the lock for the box stayed on the floor.

"I looked in the box. See what I found." He pointed to it. "A pretty shirt. But it's made funny and I can't put it on, so I brought it to Shirley. She

fixes sewed things. I want her to fix the shirt for me.
I thought if I wore it to surprise her, Dana wouldn't
mind that I got it out of her box." He looked around
at the three of them. "After I took the shirt out, I put
the lock back on the box. But, but, why isn't it okay
that I looked?" Showing an ability to reason, he said,
"Dana says we had the same momma."

Shirley said, "Dana did call yesterday morning to
ask if I could come pick Donnie up since she'd been
asked to hurry into work. Here, Henry, Donnie can't
get the shirt on, and I know you can't either. Do you
know why?"

She passed the shirt over to Henry. He turned it
inside out. "It has heavy shoulder pads and padding
around the body. Odd. Maybe if you took all that
out Donnie could wear it."

"Yes!" Donnie said.

Henry passed the shirt back to Shirley. "How
about it, can you fix it?"

"I can take the padding out. But should I? I was
thinking maybe we should go up to Dana and
Donnie's house and put it back in the Momma Box."

"NO!" Donnie said. "I want to wear it and
surprise Dana."

"She will be surprised," Carrie said.

"Can't put it back anyway," Henry reminded

them. "Donnie said he locked the box."

"Yes, locked. Lock has secret numbers."

"Okay, Donnie, I'll work on the shirt right now. Off you go to help Roger clean up in the milking barn while I remove the padding."

He hurried out the door, and for a minute none of them said anything.

"Hmm," Shirley said finally. "Are you all thinking what I'm thinking?"

"That the second thief was a woman—most likely Dana's mother?" Carrie said.

"And," Henry added, "it's interesting that the shirt was probably made for a man, then padded, so a woman wearing it would most likely be identified as male."

"Y'all wait and don't say any more," Shirley said, "I need to go get scissors and my seam rippers."

"So," she said as soon as she was back in her chair, "was the woman Dana's mother? I'd bet Dana knows—or thinks—it was, and that's why, after finding this in the rag bag, she shut down any further conversation or investigation about a red shirt. Can't say as I blame her."

"But, if she was the second person, why did her husband kill her?" Henry asked.

"Well," Shirley said, as one of the pieces of

padding from the shirt came loose, "maybe he just got too angry about something, and..."

"Or," Henry said, "for some reason he wanted to shut her up. Maybe he was concerned she would confess about the robbery, or, *wait a minute!*" Henry put his fork down on the pie plate and stayed silent for more than a minute, then he said, speaking very slowly as he thought, "Of course, all we're doing now is making up stories, and we may never know, but what if Leona Jackson was handy with a weapon. He put her in charge of killing the guards and, on purpose, she shot to wound but not to kill. Then, when Floyd Jackson found out the guards would both recover, well ..." He stopped and repeated, "We will probably never know."

* * *

Roger, Donnie, and Junior came in shortly after and, when they'd washed up, Donnie insisted on trying out his new shirt. That brought on a lot of exclamation and admiration, though it was obvious Roger and Junior were in much need of an explanation. However, after many years of marriage, Roger understood now was not the time to ask, and he was also able to squelch Junior's open-mouthed astonishment and blurted beginning questions.

Carrie stood, said she needed to get home, and

promised to call Shirley before it was time for Dana to come pick Donnie up. But, as soon as Henry had started the car, she said, "Head for Taco Mama's. We've got to warn Dana."

"What are you going to say?" he asked.

"Don't know. I'm praying for the right words."

Since both of them were full of blueberry pie, they ordered an appetizer and sat munching while Dana continued serving the only other customer in the restaurant, a man who had ordered a heaping plate of tacos. Henry murmured, "I wonder how often Dana has to put up with being stared at. She is pretty, but see, that man is watching her almost all the time. He even got her to bend over so he could whisper something to her."

"Um hum," Carrie said, "I saw, but they both laughed at whatever he said. However, I know she should be careful about that sort of thing."

When Dana came to refill their water glasses, Carrie said, "When is your next break?"

"Haven't had one yet. I came in early because two busses with a basketball team and cheerleaders arrived for a game here tonight, and they overwhelmed the first shift, so they called me for back-up. We actually just finished cleaning up after the kids. But, why do you need to know about my break?"

"Gotta talk," Carrie said. "Important."

Dana stood still for a moment, looking at Carrie, then said, "I'll clear it with the boss. Mary is finishing her break, and we're into the normal quiet time so I think it will be okay." She headed for the kitchen.

When she came back, she said, "Can we sit in your car? Boss says it doesn't look good if a server sits with customers in the dining room."

Carrie had decided telling the straight truth was best, and Henry came to the car just as she was finishing the story. He said, "Dana, do you know that man you were serving? He was asking about your home address as he checked out, and the woman helping him was wise enough to say she didn't know, but why would he be asking that? Seems suspicious to me."

"Oh, that's just Mr. Conroy. He's from Little Rock and has been working in this area for a couple of weeks. He's staying at the motel over on the highway and eats here fairly often. I'm glad Mary didn't tell him my address, but he has been nice, leaving me big tips, for one thing." She laughed. "Maybe he wanted to mail me more money."

She paused and stayed silent while Mr. Conroy left the restaurant, looked carefully at Henry's car, and then drove out of the parking lot.

"Hmm," Carrie said. "Well, I'm sure you know enough to be cautious around him."

"Okay, I only see him at the restaurant anyway. He's just a nice older man—oh, excuse me Henry. I didn't mean that like it sounded."

Henry laughed. "What you said was not offensive in any way."

"Well, okay. And besides, I just think of you two as very good friends of no particular age. Shirley and Roger now, are different. They're almost like parents to me and Donnie. So there, that's all settled. Now, Carrie, what do I do about Donnie and the shirt?"

"Admire the shirt and, if you can, let him see the contents of your mother's box. As he pointed out, she was his mother too."

Dana nodded. "I was foolish to keep it all to myself, and I will share with him now. But, legally, what about Mother being the second thief?"

Henry said, "It's sure interesting but, since she's gone, I don't see any point in discussing her part publicly, not even with Chester Blevins. I do suspect, since you said she worked part time at the City Cannery office, that—assuming she was there near the time when the payroll money was to be delivered—she was the source of inside information about the timing. Also, was she comfortable using a weapon like the robbers used? Could she have been the shooter?"

"I think she was, because I heard Daddy raging at her about those men not being dead. Please understand. I hadn't really sorted out the story until I found that shirt last night. Maybe I didn't figure it out because I didn't want to. Daddy was angry with Momma almost all the time anyway but, because of the money, the rest of our life did improve up until the day I got out of there after he killed her." Dana paused, then sighed. "I wonder now why she didn't kill him before he could kill her. I guess she didn't realize what danger she was in."

"And there were her two children to think of."

"Donnie was gone by then. Daddy had taken him away and said he left him at some home with others like him. Whether that was true or not, the county home I found him in was very nice. The state has records for places like that, and his name was on record."

"There is a problem about the shirt," Henry said. "Someone who remembers the story and is familiar with the photo at Shiloh Museum could see Donnie wearing it if he goes out in public with it on and might raise the issue publicly."

"Well, he usually doesn't go out anywhere except

to the Booths', mostly to work with Roger. Otherwise he's at our house and, sometimes, at the grocery with me. People in town are always nice to him, and they'd know he had nothing to do with the robbery."

"Okay," Carrie said. "I guess him wearing the red shirt isn't really a problem, but do be careful about it being seen in public anywhere but here in town. So, unless you have questions, that's all I had planned to talk over with you."

Dana said, "I'm glad everything is out in the open and that I wasn't the one who had to tell the story. But I hate it that Junior will learn all this. It was bad enough when he saw my Dad wearing that shirt at Shiloh. He acted nice after that, but now he'll know I have a tainted family background on both sides. He's a kind person and has done a pretty good job of continuing to act friendly but, truthfully, why would he want to get any more involved with me after this?"

"Oh, for goodness' sake, Dana. Junior lov..uh, likes you way too much to care."

"I don't think so. Since both my parents were crooks, I'm tainted, and he won't want anything to do with me."

"Nonsense."

"No, not nonsense. I do know him pretty well by

now. He's an honorable person and, I'm sure, he wants his friends to be honorable."

"What's not honorable about you?

Dana's responding laugh revealed disbelief rather than humor. "Even I can't answer that. I'm still sorting out what I think about my mother."

"Didn't she care for you as best she could?"

"As best she could? I suppose so. But here's something else—what will Roger and Shirley think of me now?"

"You should know them well enough to realize none of this history will make any difference to them."

"Hmm, maybe. But it's different with Junior because...Well, just because."

* * *

Two days later Shirley called while Carrie and Henry were cleaning up from supper. She began talking before Carrie could even say "Hello."

"Donnie stayed home all day today, and Dana just got back. He's not there."

"Oh, dear God. Oh! Is the red shirt there?"

"That's the first thing she checked, and it's gone. Can you meet Roger and me at her house now?"

"Coming."

Carrie and Henry found Shirley and Roger coping with an almost hysterical Dana in the living room.

Since the three of them were occupying her thrift-shop sofa, the only place to sit in the room, Carrie stood as they repeated exactly what Shirley had told Carrie on the phone, and Henry began a search of the house.

He was back quickly and said, "No sign of any forced entry or disruption. Would he have gone out on his own?"

"Just up to the road for the mail. I'm sure not beyond that. He understands the rules."

Henry continued, "Is Mr. Conroy still coming to the restaurant, or has there been any notable attention from anyone in town that you and Donnie have seen there recently?"

"Mr. Conroy was in Saturday and also Sunday evening. Just as friendly as he usually is. No one else."

"Was Mary on duty?"

"Not on a weekend. Goldie's back from maternity leave and is working weekends since her husband is home then and can take care of their baby."

"Could Goldie have given Mr. Conroy your home address?"

"Well, I don't know. Should I call her and ask?"

"I would," Henry said.

After a brief conversation, Dana said, "She thinks she only confirmed our road name, and he said it first. She's sure she did not mention the number."

Henry thought a moment, then said, "I suggest we go to the motel where Mr. Conroy is staying and check to see if he's still there."

"You think? Oh, no, that simply can't be!"

"Carrie and I will go check, you three can stay here."

"NO, I'm going too," Dana said.

"Then we're all coming" Shirley said. "All of us can get into our SUV."

* * *

Henry had used the folder with his Kansas City police badge fastened in it a few times since his retirement. It had been handy for gaining necessary respect or encouraging positive action when he and Carrie were working to solve a possible crime or help someone in trouble. Therefore, he stuck the badge in his pocket as he and Carrie left home that evening. When the motel desk clerk said he thought Mr. Conroy was in his room and picked up the phone to call, Henry flashed it quickly and told the clerk to put down the phone. He then asked the room number and directed a very reluctant Roger to stay with the clerk to make sure he did not notify Mr. Conroy until after the rest of them could "interview" him.

Conroy responded quickly to a knock on the door and, without opening it, said, "Who is it?"

Prompted by Henry, Dana said, "Donnie's sister." The door opened.

Dana pushed past Conroy and went to Donnie, who was sitting on a sofa in the motel suite. "Donnie, are you okay?"

"Hullo. I'm happy. Warren and I were talking about my needing a new Daddy. Warren says he would like to be my new Daddy."

"WHAT!"

Conroy said, "Just a minute. I need to tell you all something. But maybe Donnie would like to go watch the lobby's fountain pool with goldfish in it while we talk. Donnie wanted to stay there and watch the fish when we came in. Can one of you take him there?"

Donnie was already nodding, and Shirley said, "We left one of our group in the lobby. I'll take him there and be right back. But no fair talking until I get back."

"Oh, boy," Donnie said. "Is it okay, Dana?"

"Yes, and Roger is in the lobby. He'll watch the fish with you."

As soon as Shirley returned, Warren Conroy said, "So, it is Dana. Dana Jean, not Donna." He looked around at their faces, seemed encouraged, and continued. "What I am going to say now may be a shock, but it's perfectly true." After a short pause, he continued, "I am Donnie's father. If you want, DNA tests will prove it. Dana, your mother and I met when I was managing the City Canning Company. I was single—still am—and you know how things were at home for her. It wasn't long before our friendship developed into much more and, eventually, through passion more than good sense, Donnie was a result."

"But, how? When and where did you get together?"

"Not all your mother's house cleaning work was actually that. I gave her the money she supposedly took home from her work, and we spent that time together in this very motel—in this suite, in fact, though they've re-decorated completely since those long-ago days. There is a back door near here and we always used that. I even, God help me, knew about your Dad's plans for the robbery and did nothing to prevent it since I knew she was taking part, and the three of you needed the money. I even offered to distract the guards.

"I've grieved over her death all these years and have had the burden of knowing she died because your Dad found out about me."

"I can relieve you of that," Dana said. "He killed her because she had only shot to wound the guards. She was a good shot, and he had told her to kill them. He was furious because he understood she had intended to only wound them enough to put them out of commission, but not to kill. I'm sure he never knew about you, since I often heard their fights. Nothing was ever said about another man in her life. And believe me, he would have said something. Yelled it, I mean."

Warren Conroy sat on the sofa, put his head in his hands, and began to shake with sobs. Carrie and Henry sat on either side of him, and Henry laid a hand on his shoulder. Shirley put her arms around Dana, and they stood in silence until the sobs quieted.

Eventually Conroy said, "Oh, Dana, I really loved her. I wish—I wish I had taken both you and Leona away in time. By then I had found Donnie and was paying for his keep in a good place. But you and Leona—well, I didn't save her, and I thought you were dead, too."

"What about Donnie?"

"Last time I went to the home where he was living, they said his sister had taken him to live with her, and since I had never revealed to them that I was his birth father, they released him to you and were pretty careful about sharing more information. Someone did say your road's name, and I remembered that from before. Leona and I had driven down your road once, and she pointed out the lane to your house. The fact that the motel where Leona and I spent so much time was not too far away helped confirm the location. I have money in investments and also a good pension, so I decided to leave my job in Little Rock and come here, hoping to find Donnie—and you. I was lucky enough to see you at Taco Mama's and wondered if you might be Dana. There is some family resemblance, and I figured you could be using a different name for your own reasons. When the lady at the restaurant confirmed your road's name, I just had to see if I had finally located my son. When he came for the mail, well, the need to be with him overwhelmed me. I supposed you'd be on duty until the restaurant closed, and I intended to go back with Donnie by then and tell you all that I am telling you now."

"W H E W," said Shirley.

* * *

Two months later, Warren and Junior came into Shirley's kitchen for a lunch that Carrie and Henry had brought to share. "How's the remodel job coming?" Carrie asked.

"Well," Warren said, "Junior knows what he's doing, and I guess I'm good at listening to and following directions. We've almost finished modernizing the kitchen, and the appliances I ordered are in place and actually working." He smiled. "Pretty soon Junior, Dana, Donnie, and I can attempt a family dinner for you all, though I do hesitate, knowing full well we are living in the shadow of Shirley's talents in the kitchen."

"Don't let that stop you," Carrie said. "I made the tuna salad for the sandwiches you guys are having for lunch, and I think it's pretty good."

"It's real good," Shirley said. "Somehow my tuna salad never tastes as good as yours."

"You don't put enough sweet pickle relish in it," Carrie said. "And, truth to tell, I think even the cheapest pickle relish off the grocery shelf makes a better tuna salad than your home-made."

"Well, my gracious," Shirley said. "I'll look for the kind you get in the store and try it out. Never believed bought would outdo homemade, though."

"We find good things many places," Carrie said.

Henry laughed. "Words of wisdom, from a sometimes cook. That is, if you can call tuna salad cooked."

Carrie swatted him with her napkin. "The hard-boiled eggs in it are cooked."

"I'll remember to tell Dana about store-bought pickle relish," Shirley said. "I've been teaching her to cook on her day off. You might want to try her meatloaf for your first meal in her new kitchen."

Junior said, "*Meatloaf?* I want to marry that woman."

"Well, why don't you?"

"Oh! Sorry, I blurted that out. She is polite to me and very grateful for the updates in her house, thanks to Warren's money and my skills. But beyond that, nothing. She avoids any close contact and won't accept what I'd call a date with me. If she won't go out with me, why wouldn't she just laugh at any suggestion about us getting married? I can't handle the possibility she would laugh and say no, thus crashing any small hopes I might have about the two of us standing up in front of a preacher someday."

Warren said, "She'll say yes. You may be good at house remodeling, but maybe you aren't so good at loving a woman and knowing how she feels about things. As a bachelor who has only loved one woman in his life, I am sure I can say that Dana Jean is very much in love with you." He paused, looked at his plate, then said softly, "I knew her mother loved me."

Junior stared at him. "You think Dana would

agree to marrying with me?"

"You bet I do. Don't let her father win a battle against real love from his grave."

Shirley set a plate of cookies in the center of the table and said, "Junior Booth, I'm your momma and until now, I didn't know you could blush.

"But listen to Warren, and now to me. I think a big problem is that Dana thinks her past is a roadblock to future happiness with you. She thinks you might always remember how awful her family life was, and about the robbery and all, and that would lead to eventual hate, or at least a lack of respect as your main feeling for her."

"That's crazy."

"Don't say that. Just stop and try to think inside her head. What do you say, Warren, knowing her mother so well and all?"

"Junior, your mother is right. Take her words to heart."

"So, it's what happened with her father, maybe her mother too, and not her personal dislike for me that's the problem? Ah. Well then, somehow, I've gotta make her understand that I truly, really, love her, and I'm not gonna let her father win a battle against real love. How am I supposed to do that?"

"Talk in real feelings, not made-up words. Talk

like you have just done with us. And maybe I can help a bit. I have your grandma's wedding ring. I'll give it to you to give Dana when you ask her to be your wife. I know it's not like a fancy engagement ring, but it has beautiful memories and is a family treasure. That ought to help convince her."

* * *

"Isn't that just the best meal you've ever eaten?" Junior said, as all eight of them sat at Dana's new dining table.

He stood up. "And I want our friends here to know that Dana Jean Jackson agreed to marry with me while we were both peeling potatoes and, I tell you, it's a wonder the mashed potatoes and meatloaf you just ate ever got made. Anyway, Dana may make the best meatloaf on earth, but it could taste like dog food and I would still love her forever."

"Oh, Junior," Dana said, "when did you ever eat dog food?"

"Let's see," Shirley mused. "I think he was around three."

After the laughter, Donnie's "Hooo-ray" punctuated happy exclamations.

Suddenly Shirley was all business. "Okay, Dana. On your next day off, we measure you for the wedding dress I'm gonna make for you. You can look at Carrie's wedding dress some evening between now and then so you can see I do a pretty good job at such things. I also made both our girls' wedding dresses. They each took theirs with them when they moved away, but I've got pictures. In the meantime, do you have any requests?"

Dana, looking dreamy, said, "Lace. I'd like something with lace."

"Lace? You betcha."

ABOUT THE AUTHOR

Radine Trees Nehring's award-winning writing career began when she fell in love with the Arkansas Ozarks and wanted to tell people why. Her essays and feature articles about the people, places, and events in her adopted state began selling almost immediately to magazines and newspapers. The first book in her Carrie and Henry "To Die For" amateur detective series came out in 2002, rapidly drawing fans into the mysterious Ozarks. "Solving Peculiar Crimes" adds intriguing and unique Carrie and Henry short stories to that series. Radine is a member of Sisters in Crime, Mystery Writers of America, and Authors Guild. She was the chosen inductee into the Arkansas Writers Hall of Fame in 2011.

Visit Radine's website (www.RadinesBooks.com) for Carrie's recipes, Radine's other books, and more.

A VALLEY TO DIE FOR

Carrie and Henry come to the Ozarks on separate quests. What they find is murder!

2003 Macavity Award Nominee

MUSIC TO DIE FOR

Carrie and Henry's special vacation is cancelled by kidnapping and murder.

A TREASURE TO DIE FOR

An Elderhostel at Hot Springs, Arkansas, is turned upside down when Carrie disappears in steaming water and Henry goes hunting.

A WEDDING TO DIE FOR

Carrie and Henry's wedding at the Crescent Hotel in Eureka Springs, Arkansas, is threatened by a bombing, a murder, and a ghost bride wearing red.

Chosen by the Arkansas Center for the Book and the Arkansas State Library as a best book, 2006

A RIVER TO DIE FOR

Carrie gets cranky about camping with Henry and "the kids" until Catherine and Rob find danger in the caves of Arkansas's Buffalo National River.

JOURNEY TO DIE FOR
Carrie and Henry take a train ride into danger, deception, and death.

Winner of the 2010 Silver Falchion
award at Killer Nashville

A FAIR TO DIE FOR
Thousands visit the War Eagle area of Arkansas expecting good things. Not hidden identities. Not murder.

A PORTRAIT TO DIE FOR
Art crime so well hidden that no one suspects— until Carrie McCrite and an aggressive reporter notice something odd in two portraits of twins.

DEAR EARTH: A LOVE LETTER FROM SPRING HOLLOW
A heart-warming true adventure about love and learning, sorrows and joys, and also a practical guide to what life in the country can be like for a city-born couple who left it all—and found their dreams.

Winner of almost a dozen writing awards

CPSIA information can be obtained
at www.ICGtesting.com
Printed in the USA
FSHW021353081120